MATTERS OF THE HEART

Other titles by Kathy J. Jacobson:

In the Secret Heart

A Change of Heart

MATTERS OF THE HEART

KATHY J. JACOBSON

atmosphere press

© 2025 Kathy J. Jacobson

Published by Atmosphere Press

Cover design by Matthew Fielder

No part of this book may be reproduced without permission from the author except in brief quotations and in reviews. This is a work of fiction, and any resemblance to real places, persons, or events is entirely coincidental.

Atmospherepress.com

For hearts needing hope

Chapter 1

Valentine's Day

Sergeant Joe Zimmerman maneuvered his squad car slowly down the main street of Farmerton, taking in the decorated streetlamps and windows of the downtown businesses. Hearts of red and pink had been painted on windows by the middle- and high-school art class students. Newly hung LED heart lights were ablaze, helping brighten the main thoroughfare on this frosty, gray day. Even though it was dreary and cold outside, the atmosphere in town on this special day was one of welcome and warmth.

Most small towns concentrated on Christmas adornments, but not this tiny rural village in Wisconsin. Instead, Farmerton went "all out" for Valentine's Day, a tradition that began with the first Fireman's Valentine's Day Ball fifty years before. Being a special anniversary this year, Farmerton was determined to make this the best and most memorable celebration yet.

Now the occasion was officially titled the Farmerton Area Fire and Rescue Squad Valentine's Day Dance and Auction. Even so, many community members still insisted on using its former name, especially those citizens who had been residents at its inception.

Ever since its inaugural year, people traveled from all over the county, dressed in their best and ready to dance to a live band on the Friday night prior to Valentine's Day, or on the very day when it fell on a Friday, as it did this year. A few years back, someone had dared to suggest they use a DJ instead of a band, and the person had almost been run out of town. Nothing could replace a live band.

As the event gained popularity over the years, the auction had been added, which brought in even more people, which meant more funds for the department. Many people bid on the donated items. Others enjoyed the all-you-can-eat appetizers, desserts, coffee, and punch. Area businesses and organizations were very generous in their donations and enjoyed friendly competition with one another, so the donations and food offerings improved every year. No one did Valentine's Day like Farmerton. It was *the* place to be, and the highlight of the year for its residents.

As Joe continued down the street, he could almost feel the excitement and anticipation in the air as the dance was only hours away. He glanced ahead at the feed mill at the end of the street. It had a huge heart on its cupula, emblazoned in red lights like a beacon directing people into town.

But it wasn't only Farmerton that was filled with excitement and anticipation. Joe and his wife, Jodie, had everyone beat in that category. They were about to become first-time parents. Their baby was due in the middle of March, now only a month away. Joe thought about the unassembled white wooden crib leaning against the wall, ready to be put together and set up in the nursery. That would be his project the next day.

At least he had painted the walls of the room the prior weekend. Jodie had chosen a warm, pale green shade called "Meadow." She added some simple woodland art decals on the wall as soon as the paint was dry. She had wished she could have helped Joe paint, but had chosen to stay away from the fumes.

Jodie had been doing everything by the book so far in this pregnancy and wasn't going to change that now. She was very excited to become a mom, but she also admitted to counting down the days until she could "get her body back." She wanted to ski and do her hard-core workout routines once again. She also craved a glass of red wine, which she planned to imbibe in celebration upon the birth of their child.

They had chosen both a boy and a girl name, having decided to be surprised when the baby came instead of learning the gender ahead of time. So, bit by bit, things were coming together. Still, that didn't quell the feelings of inadequacy—and occasionally of sheer panic—they both experienced, especially Joe. Joe had a lot of questions in his heart. Was he really father material? His first marriage shortly out of high school had been an absolute disaster. His subsequent relationships were short-lived and unfulfilling. He hadn't met Jodie until his late thirties and married her when he was forty years old.

His thoughts drifted toward his father. His dad had been a good father, but his father's father, Joe's paternal grandfather, had been an unkind and abusive man. Joe hoped he would not inherit any of his grandfather's personal traits.

Joe's recent volunteer work with the high-school football team, along with mentoring for a few years now one of its former stars, Rowdy Reynolds, had helped Joe gain some confidence in dealing with young people. Still, teenagers were not babies. Joe thought about how he had only changed a diaper once in his life—his niece's—and that was a long time ago. And feeding a baby a bottle—he had no experience whatsoever. Jodie had received some bottles at a recent shower thrown for her. He had studied the pamphlet that came with them—they were supposed to be the best bottles for most babies—like he was going to take a final exam. Afterward, he watched a video on his computer about the best positions to hold a newborn baby during a feeding. Joe was taking parenting very seriously.

Joe had no idea that there was so much information to take in concerning the raising of a child. And then there was the massive quantity of baby items they had accumulated, which had filled the nursery closet and been stacked up in a corner. It was incredible. How could one small human need so many things?

Joe tried to concentrate on the holiday decorations and his love for Jodie instead of his growing anxiety. He was looking forward to the dance and sharing an evening with his beautiful wife. She was the best thing that had ever happened to him, and he knew how very fortunate he was. He also knew they would make this parent thing work. He just wanted to make sure he got his part right.

He threw his head back against the headrest of the vehicle and sighed, but then smiled as he parked his squad in front of Sissy's Scissors to get a trim for the evening's grand event. Sissy always made him feel better about anything and everything.

Sissy threw the chartreuse cape around Sgt. Joe Zimmerman's shoulders as he sat in the chair at Sissy's

Scissors, the beauty salon on Main Street. He needed a little "clean-up," as Sissy called it, before the big dance. Apparently, he wasn't the only one, as all three chairs in the small downtown shop were occupied. Three women sat waiting for their turns, and the phone was constantly ringing, much to the chagrin of the other two hairstylists, who took turns answering it. Over and over, they delivered the disappointing news that they were completely booked for the rest of the day.

The usually bubbly Sissy looked tired, which was very unlike her. She was one of the most cheerful and positive people Joe knew.

"Everything all right, Sissy?" Joe asked.

"Oh, it's just been a very busy week," she said unconvincingly. She worked quietly, which was also unlike her. Sissy was extremely skilled with her scissors and quickly trimmed his hair. No one else could work magic with Joe's hair like Sissy. She brushed the loose hair from the cape and turned Joe around in the chair to face the mirror. "You're good to go, Joe."

He stood up and handed her money, which she didn't even try to refuse like she usually did. Even though he never took "freebies," she usually gave him more of an argument about him paying her for a haircut.

"I'll see you tonight at the dance?" he asked.

"If I'm still alive, I'll be there," she said tiredly.

Joe smiled, and Sissy forced a smile back at him.

Joe walked briskly to his squad as a blast of icy air met his face, the temperature outside a sharp contrast to that of the cozy salon. He thought about Sissy's demeanor and hoped she was truly okay. Sissy was one of Joe's favorite people in town. She was kind, caring, generous, and funny, but she truly hadn't been herself today. Of course, she was not wrong about it having been a very busy week. He was certain the shop had been packed with customers every single day leading up to the big dance and auction.

Joe didn't have much time to dwell on his thoughts as his phone rang. He jumped into the squad, started the engine, and checked his phone. It indicated the call was from his friend, Simon. Simon had become one of his closest friends, a development surprising to both men. Joe had arrested Simon for driving while intoxicated and crashing his vehicle. Joe had convinced Simon that he could turn his life around if he were to go to rehab and do some serious work. Simon did, and his life had changed almost more dramatically than Joe's. Not only had Simon been sober for almost five years, but he was also a happily married man and had become incredibly successful in his real estate development business.

He'd built a beautiful home in the country and had fallen in love with a business acquaintance. Now, Simon and his wife, Sally, were trying desperately to have a child, but had no success over the past year and a half. They had recently completed another round of medical tests, along with filling out paperwork to adopt a child.

Joe pushed the icon to accept the call, hoping Simon had some good news to share.

"Hey, Simon," Joe answered cheerfully.

"Hi, Joe," Simon said.

"What can I do for you?"

"Feel free to say no to this, but would you mind filling out a recommendation form for us—actually, for me—to the adoption agency? They already have one from the pastor and from my sister, but I think yours might be more helpful. I know you've seen me at my worst, but you've also seen me at my best, and I think your word could carry some weight," he said.

"Of course. Send it to me and I'll do it right away," Joe said. He was proud of Simon for his dedication to staying in recovery. It was hard at times to even remember the blindly intoxicated man Joe had arrested after a near-tragic one-car crash into a tree. Simon's life had been in shambles in so many ways at that time, which was no longer the case.

"We would really appreciate it, Joe. It might be our best bet to become parents—our test results aren't sounding very encouraging, unfortunately," Simon said sadly.

"Sorry to hear that, Simon." Joe didn't say more. He knew that Simon blamed their lack of success in getting pregnant on his years of heavy drinking. "Just give me the specifics and I'll get right on it."

"Thanks, friend. You're the best," Simon responded.

"See you tonight?" Joe asked.

"Yes, we wouldn't miss it. The fire and rescue department deserves everyone's support. Plus, it will be a good diversion from..." Simon couldn't go on.

"Right," said Joe. "We'll see you tonight."

They hung up at the same time. Joe felt bad for Simon and Sally, especially for Simon. He didn't know how much Simon's former drinking habit could affect his ability to father a child, but he knew that Simon felt it did. Simon was feeling a lot of guilt and remorse these days.

Joe's stomach growled, so he decided to head to Bud's Diner for lunch. A bowl of Bud's famous chili—one of Joe's favorite foods—sounded like perfection to him. Just the thought of the spicy delight made Joe's mouth water, and he hurried down the street to the diner.

Bud's Diner was swarming with customers, with all the tables and booths occupied. Luckily, there was one open stool at the counter for Joe. Two waitresses, Bud, and another cook were churning out orders as fast as they could. Apparently, Joe wasn't the only one who thought Bud's chili would be a good idea on a day like this. The thick, steamy chili, served with Bud's homemade cornbread, were the most popular items on the menu. Joe and Jodie had even had them served at their wedding dinner on a frosty New Year's Day two years ago.

Joe slid onto the stool and ordered a bowl, reluctantly passing on the cornbread this time. Ever since he found out he was going to be a parent, he had been even more diligent about eating well and exercising. He wanted to be around to see his child grow into an adult and was more motivated than ever to live a healthy lifestyle. He worked out every day, even though he'd had to move his equipment to an area in the basement, as the baby's room had formerly been his workout room.

Joe's order came quickly. He crumbled some soda crackers into the thick liquid and stirred, watching the steam rise from the heavy white ceramic bowl. He set his spoon down for a minute to let the soup cool off, listening to the conversations around him. Bud's was second only to Sissy's Scissors for all the town "news."

There was a table behind Joe where four men were seated. Each one was dressed in blue jeans, a flannel shirt, and a baseball cap. Three of them worked at the feed mill, and the other was a farmer named Clifford, a longtime bachelor who had recently started coming to church at St.

John's, the church Joe and Jodie attended. The farmer was being teased by one of the other men.

"So, you going to the dance tonight, Cliffy? I hear your sweetie is going to be there this year," the man said gleefully.

Clifford turned a bright shade of scarlet. "I don't know what you're talking about," he said in a defensive tone.

"I saw you giving her eggs last Sunday after church."

"I've got eggs coming out of my ears this winter—I had to do something with them," Clifford answered.

"Well, I don't see you bringing me any," the man retorted.

"Aw, let him alone," another man said.

Just then, the table fell silent as their bowls of chili and a plate of warm cornbread arrived, saving Clifford from further embarrassment.

Joe wondered who this supposed "sweetie" was. It appeared that it must be one of the church members. He hadn't seen Clifford after the service, as Joe had been busy helping count the offering, serving as a substitute for one of the regular counters who had stayed home with a nasty cold. It was the height of cold and flu season in the Midwest, one of the worst aspects of the long winter season.

Joe turned his attention back to his lunch and took a few bites of the chili, which was now at the perfect temperature. It was spectacular, as usual. Also, as usual, Joe's meal was interrupted. This time the culprit was an emergency call, which kicked off a week he would never forget as long as he lived.

Chapter 2

Margaret Miller's eyes had been as big as saucers when a flower delivery was made to the church office at St. John's. The young delivery man with ruddy cheeks and a runny nose had been cheerful, even though he had been working since early in the morning in the bitter cold and still had more stops to make in Farmerton and several other communities in the area. It was the busiest day of the year for the flower shop—actually, for every flower seller in the nation. The young man knew he would be receiving bonus pay on this day, along with occasional tips, which kept a tiny smile on his face; otherwise, he would have been cursing about how miserable he felt.

His hands were stiff and as cold as ice, but his chest and armpits were sweaty from hustling to and from his van to his delivery destinations. Even though he was wearing hiking boots, his feet were wet, as were the bottoms of his jeans, as snow kept blowing and drifting over walkways and parking lots. His red hands matched his face, and his eyes were so watery that Margaret considered asking him if something was wrong. He was sniffling as he handed her the large bouquet, which was encased in stiff, clear plastic to protect the flowers from the sub-zero temperature outside. After handing her the flowers, he instinctively wiped his nose with his coat sleeve, then practically ran out the door as it was apparent there would be no tip at this stop.

Margaret looked at the attached envelope and read the

name. For a fleeting moment, she had let herself believe that the deep red, long-stemmed roses inside the protective wrap could be for her, but as was typical, they were for someone else. This time the recipient was the interim pastor at St. John's, Pastor Kate, who had been serving the congregation for a few years now, ever since the former pastor had died—actually, been murdered, although Margaret had never truly been able to come to grips with the reality of that awful fact.

Margaret wanted so badly to smell the roses, but they weren't hers to smell. After the young man bolted out the door, she gazed at the beautiful flowers for a moment, then stood up from her desk and walked to the closed door between her secretary's office and the pastor's study, knocking lightly. A moment later, the door opened to Pastor Kate's smiling face. Her bright blue eyes sparkled, and her cheeks had their usual rosy glow, making her resemble how Margaret imagined an angel might look.

Margaret, who had worked in the office for more than twenty-five years, had not been thrilled initially with the prospect of a female pastor, but it was difficult to dislike Pastor Kate. She was kind and easygoing, yet strong when she needed to be. She had successfully pulled a torn and tattered congregation back together at an incredibly difficult time, but then again, that was why she had been assigned as an interim at St. John's. Short-term, difficult assignments had been the pastor's life work for the past twenty years, with nearly as many assignments in that span of time. St. John's was by far the longest position she had held, due to the gravity of the situation and also the dearth of people willing to take such assignments.

Most of Pastor Kate's "calls" had been to places where

there had been inappropriate relationships between a pastor and a church member, usually of a sexual nature. Not only had St. John's experienced this between their pastor and church choir director, but both ended up being murdered because of it. The events caused incredible pain for the congregation and the entire community of Farmerton, but Pastor Kate had skillfully tended to the wounds, and things finally felt normal and peaceful again.

The pastor took the roses from Margaret and removed the cold, crinkly wrap, which had started to fog up inside the toasty office. She carefully peeled off a small envelope that had been taped to the outside.

"I wonder who could have sent these beauties?" she asked out loud.

Kate opened the envelope and took out a small white card. She unfolded it and read the single bold-typed word on the inside. Her eyes grew even larger than Margaret's had at the sight of the flowers, and then her face became ashen. She gasped, then crumpled to the floor in a heap.

Margaret had immediately called 9-1-1 and could hear a siren in the distance as she covered the pastor with her old, navy-blue wool coat. She was happy the pastor appeared to be breathing on her own and had a pulse, as Margaret wasn't sure she remembered the finer points of the CPR class she had taken many years before.

The first one on the scene was Sgt. Joe Zimmerman, who came bursting into the office, the rescue squad not far behind. Pastor Kate had begun to stir and tried to sit up. Joe made her lay back down until the trained professionals had done an assessment of her condition.

After a check of her pulse and with some color returning to the pastor's face, Joe and a responder helped her sit upright. Kate's complexion quickly blossomed into a dark shade of crimson. She was not used to being "ministered to" in any way. She was usually the one holding someone else's hand and comforting them, not the other way around. She could barely stand all the fuss going on around her and couldn't wait until the embarrassing situation was over, wondering how many of her parishioners had already heard of the emergency at the church. And then she thought about how many questions she would have to field about this situation between now and Sunday morning.

The EMT checked her blood pressure and gave her water to drink, then asked her questions about her general health. No, she didn't take any medications. No, she didn't have any chronic health problems. Yes, she had eaten a good breakfast and lunch, but no, she hadn't had a lot of water to drink. No, nothing like this had ever happened to her before. Yes, she had a doctor and would follow up with her as soon as possible and promised to drink water steadily the rest of the day.

Joe and another responder helped the pastor to her feet, watching to make certain she was truly steady. When enough time had passed, the squad packed up their medical supplies and headed out, grateful that they didn't have to race to the hospital on the wintry roads or, even worse, possibly miss out on the upcoming festivities in Farmerton that evening.

Tonight was their big night—the dance and auction—a huge fundraiser for their department. Not only did they enjoy the fun event, but they had the opportunity to make enough money to make their equipment "wish list" become a reality. They hoped to break last year's record attendance and donation records, and were excited that, while it might be cold, there was no bad weather predicted until late the next night. They should have a good turnout again this year.

"Margaret, thank you so much for your help," Pastor Kate said sincerely after the office had cleared.

"You really gave me a scare," Margaret answered, visibly shaken.

"I think you should take the rest of the afternoon off. Don't worry, you can still put down your regular hours on your timesheet," the pastor said.

"Are you sure, Pastor?" Margaret asked.

"I'm sure. I'm good now—in fact, I think we both should go home and start getting ready for the dance tonight."

Margaret smiled. "I'll see you there, Pastor Kate. I'm so glad you are okay," she added sincerely.

"Me, too," Pastor Kate said, faking a smile.

She watched Margaret pick up her wool coat from the floor, then log out of her desktop computer for the day. Everything was set for Sunday days ago, as Margaret was always working ahead on one thing or another. The pastor had never had such an efficient secretary before—almost too efficient at times, as it was difficult to make any last-minute adjustments with Margaret doing the bulletins.

Margaret waved to the pastor as she started to exit the office. Pastor Kate pretended to be getting her own coat to go home, but as soon as Margaret was out of sight, Kate sat down at her desk, where Margaret had put the bouquet of roses and the card.

Kate opened the card and read it once more. Then she crumpled it up, put on her coat, picked up the flowers, and made doubly certain the office and outer doors were locked on her way out. As she made her way to her car in the church parking lot, she stopped at the trash dumpster and pitched the card and roses into it, the top of the heavy metal lid clanging down loudly as it closed.

Kate got into her car, feeling like a zombie. She thought about the week she'd had, and suddenly felt afraid. Several unusual things had transpired, but she hadn't given them an extra thought until now. She remembered how her garbage can had apparently blown over sometime Saturday night or very early on Sunday, its contents scattering all over her front lawn when she got up to go to St. John's.

Then, after church, when she was finally ready to leave the building after the service on Sunday, she found she had a flat tire. She had called for roadside assistance, which took an extra-long time on a Sunday. The man checked over the tire, finding no good reason as to why it had lost its air. He inflated the tire with a portable air compressor. He had been so thrilled that he could quickly get back to his son's wrestling match that he hadn't even charged her for the call.

But worst of all, she had lost her favorite scarf, one of the last items she owned that had been knitted by her mother.

Kate sighed. She didn't have time to dwell on such things. She needed to go home and get ready for the biggest social event of the year in Farmerton, which felt as inviting to her as a root canal. She knew she had to attend, though. The rumors would only grow more sensational if she didn't show up for the dance. She envisioned how Bud's Diner, Sissy's Scissors, and even the feed mill would already be humming with theories about her collapse. Hopefully, she could throw some water on the flames before they got too out of hand with a simple appearance at the evening's event.

Kate started the car's engine and just sat for a few minutes, staring at the church building. She knew she had taken a risk staying in one place for this long. She turned the ignition, and the vehicle started with a long, slow whine. She let out a sigh. *Your past is finally catching up with you, Kate.* Unfortunately, even though she had her suspicions, she wasn't completely certain which part of her past it was, a thought that plagued her as she put the car in gear and crept out of the parking lot.

Chapter 3

The Night of the Dance

Jodie looked into the full-length mirror and smoothed the soft, burgundy-colored dress around her bulging midsection. She smiled a huge smile, which widened even more when she saw Joe's reflection appear next to hers. She felt his strong hands slide around her from behind and hold her firmly yet gently. He nuzzled her ear, which Joe knew drove her crazy.

"Joe, we don't want to be late," she said.

"Are you sure about that?" Joe asked as he kissed her neck. Joe thought Jodie had never looked more intoxicatingly beautiful than she currently did in her last trimester of pregnancy.

She laughed and turned toward him, putting her arms around his neck and grinning up at him.

"As tempting as it is, I believe you are one of the auctioneers tonight, and we don't want to disappoint the fire chief."

"As usual, you are annoyingly correct, but let's pick up where we left off when we get home later," he said, sounding hopeful.

"Deal," she said, knowing full well that she would be much too tired by the time they got home, even if they left early. She hadn't gone to bed so early on a regular basis since she was in the eighth grade. "Plus," Jodie added, "I have to see for myself that Pastor Kate is okay."

The pastor had become very important to both Joe and Jodie in the past year or so. Not only had Kate officiated their marriage, but she had served as one of Jodie's counselors in the aftermath of her scary abduction by a troubled young man the year before. The pastor had also referred Jodie to an amazing therapist, whom she still saw from time to time.

Joe was anxious to see the pastor, too. There was something still bothering him about the entire situation at the church earlier in the day. He was sure there was more to the story. Something was going on, but he had nothing to go on except his gut instinct. Maybe he would have an opportunity to speak with the pastor at some point in the evening and he would feel better, but that never happened.

Pastor Kate looked at the disappointing wardrobe in her closet. What could she possibly wear to a dance? Maybe a better question was what did a pastor wear to a Valentine's dance? Her selection of suits, clerical shirts, and collars was not going to cut it this time.

Kate had little desire to go to this event in the first place, but she had passed on it the two years before and had never heard the end of it. Every couple in the church, along with almost the entire community of Farmerton and neighboring towns' residents, attended.

She knew it would be a wonderful place to connect with people, and of course it was a fundraiser for a very good cause. But why did it have to be a Valentine's Day event? Kate usually tried to block out every aspect of this holiday, as it brought back too many memories. She sighed deeply and took out a simple black dress she had forgotten she owned. She held it up to herself in the mirror and was transported back in time. Her eyes misted as she unsuccessfully tried to shake off a memory.

She quickly dressed, ran a comb through her hair, then hurried to her car. Thankfully, it was parked in the garage of the parsonage, so she didn't have to scrape off any frost. Her plan was to make an appearance, bid on some item she really didn't need that she would later donate or give away as a gift. She would stay for the least amount of time she could get away with, then come home and watch a movie. Maybe she'd even have a glass of wine with her movie, which always relaxed her. And she needed to relax after the events of the day, which despite her best efforts were impossible to dismiss. Maybe the dance would be a good diversion, she thought as she started her car and headed out for the evening.

The gymnasium at Farmerton High School was filled with an impressive display of helium balloons, streamers, and lights. A live six-piece band and a singer had assembled on the stage, which ran parallel to the basketball court. The stage was used for the pep band during basketball games, as well as concerts and the annual play, as auditoriums were very rare in small rural schools like the one in Farmerton. Dance music would play between auction sessions, the items for bidding growing bigger and better as the evening progressed.

People were in a festive mood and dressed for the

occasion. The women tended toward dressing in shades of red, although black certainly had its presence, making Kate feel more comfortable about her attire. The men wore suits and ties. For many of them, it was the only time they donned such apparel all year.

Kate spied Joe and Jodie. Usually, she would have gone straight over to talk to the couple, who had become very dear to her, but tonight, she felt like avoiding Joe and any reminders of the emergency call earlier in the day. Of course, there was no way to avoid the subject entirely, as every person she knew began by asking her how she was feeling the moment she stepped through the door. She was happy when the auction and dance numbers began and there were fewer occasions for dialogue.

In addition to the live auction, a silent auction was in progress, which was more Kate's style. Earlier in the week she had considered bidding on one of the larger live-auction items she had read about in the newspaper, but now she didn't want to call attention to herself, so that plan was out. Bidding with an anonymous number was fun and much more discreet. She kept circling back to a soft and fashionable fleece scarf and gloves set from Lands' End, upping her bid each time she was outbid. She decided she actually needed a new scarf, considering her favorite was either lost or misplaced. Kate would be absent by the time they announced the winning bids at the end of the evening, so she most likely wouldn't win them, but at least she knew she had helped raise the ante.

Kate was getting thirsty and headed to the refreshment table for some water. A volunteer handed her a glass and she thanked the woman. She turned around with a plastic cup in her hand and found herself face-to-face with Joe.

"If I didn't know any better, I'd think you were avoiding me," he said, looking her straight in the eye.

Kate didn't know how to respond, so she didn't say anything.

"I was thinking about today," Joe went on, "wondering what really happened."

"What do you mean, Joe? I just fainted," she said, which was at least in part the truth.

"There you are!" Jodie arrived at their sides, giving Pastor Kate a reprieve from the conversation with Joe.

"Jodie, look at you!" Pastor Kate said. "You are glowing."

"And you look well, Pastor. You must be feeling better," Jodie responded. Pastor Kate started to blush and looked uncomfortable, so Jodie changed the subject. "I like your dress. I don't think I've ever seen you in one before."

"There are not many occasions to wear one in my line of work," Kate responded.

"I know what you mean," Jodie said. "I enjoy wearing something other than my usual, too," she said, referring to her uniform as a sheriff's deputy. That was how Jodie and Joe had ended up together. They were colleagues first, then friends, later lovers, and now spouses about to become first-time parents.

"Well, you look very nice," Jodie said, giving the woman's arm a squeeze.

"Thank you, Jodie. I appreciate your approval," Kate said, thankful she had found the old dress.

"Oh, excuse me," Jodie said suddenly. "Nature calls. This baby has me running to the restroom every fifteen minutes these days."

Joe and Pastor Kate watched Jodie as she walked

quickly out of the gym and turned to go down the hallway to the restroom.

"She really does look great, Joe. And the baby—all is well?"

"Yes, and yes, but nice redirection, Pastor Kate," he said. "You know, I expect to be lied to on a fairly regular basis by the people I question—but I just never expected my pastor to be one of them," Joe said seriously.

"I don't know what you mean," Pastor Kate started to say, but was saved as the music started up once more.

People began dancing, and the talking stopped. Kate was going to take a sip of her water when suddenly there was a very loud sound. Joe knew that distinctive sound, the sound of a shot being fired. Then another one rang out.

He looked at the gym door, the one Jodie had gone through just moments before. He glimpsed the backside of a person dressed from head to toe in all-black clothing and a ski mask running out of the building.

"Everyone, get down!" Joe yelled.

The music stopped abruptly, and chaos ensued. Everyone was screaming and taking cover as Joe prepared to pursue the perpetrator. First, he turned to see if Pastor Kate was okay, but she wasn't standing next to him anymore. Then he looked down, and there she was. She had been wounded. He quickly waved over one of the many EMTs in attendance, then flew to the door of the gym and out to the parking lot in pursuit of the fleeing shooter.

He saw a dark vehicle speed out of the lot, but he couldn't quite decipher the make or model and didn't see a license plate. They needed to improve the lighting in the school parking lot, for certain. He called in the event to the dispatcher and gave them what little information he had about the shooter and the escape vehicle. The dispatcher had already been advised of the shooting by someone on the rescue squad who was also in attendance at the event. Then Joe's thoughts turned to Jodie, and he rushed back inside the building.

Joe's heart pounded wildly with fear. Luckily, he heard Jodie's voice calling his name as he stepped through the entrance to the school. She had been even more frightened than he was, knowing that he had pursued the shooter into the night.

They ran into each other's arms and held one another tightly, their eyes conveying looks of concern and love.

"Is anyone hurt?" Jodie asked.

"Unfortunately, yes," he answered. Joe hesitated, not wanting to upset his very pregnant wife, but knew she had to know.

"Pastor Kate was wounded," he said as calmly as possible, holding Jodie's arm tightly.

Upon hearing this, Jodie rushed into the gym, followed closely by Joe. Jodie carefully lowered herself down to Pastor Kate's side, where a responder was tending to her for the second time that day. This woman had done so much for her after her traumatic experience of the past. And with Jodie's parents still living on the other side of the state, she sometimes saw the pastor as a parental figure in her life.

Jodie spoke to Kate, reassuring her, even though she was unconscious. The first responder was applying direct pressure with his shirt to a chest wound, and a towel had been placed under the pastor's head. Another responder covered her with a blanket that had been a part of the silent auction items, trying to keep her from going into shock.

Another rescue squad member came into the gym with a gurney from the ambulance that had thankfully been parked outside the gym in the parking lot. They usually did this to remind the attendees what this evening was all about, and because almost every first responder in the county was in attendance. This was the first time it had ever been used during a dance.

Together the responders helped get the pastor onto the gurney and escorted her outside to the waiting ambulance. They would be transporting her to the University of Wisconsin Hospital in Madison, the nearest hospital equipped to handle gunshot wounds.

Joe and Jodie, along with several other officers who had just arrived, got to work calming people down, taking statements, and helping the anxious organizers of the event. It was decided that once the police were done speaking with each person, everyone should go to their homes and lock their doors, as the shooter was still not in custody.

The youth wrestling event scheduled for the following afternoon in the gym would have to be postponed, as it was now considered an active crime scene. Everything would stay in its place until the officers gave them clearance to leave and their names were put on a list, with any statements recorded.

The auction items would stay where they were, too, including those that had already been won. The organizers met in a corner of the gym. They planned to meet the next day to decide how to handle the remainder of the auction. Hundreds of individuals and businesses had donated to this important fundraiser, and no one wanted to let the rescue squad down. They needed to come up with an alternative plan.

Joe finally convinced Jodie to catch a ride home with another deputy and said he would be there shortly. He was looking for something. Joe had heard two shots, and there was only one person wounded without an exit wound. He was quite certain there was a bullet lodged somewhere in the gym. He put several other deputies on a hunt for a possible bullet hole, or anything that looked like it had possibly been damaged by a bullet, but no one found anything.

Finally, Joe returned to the exact spot where he and Pastor Kate had been standing when the shots were fired. He turned around and scanned the area behind him. At first, he didn't see anything, but then he noticed a tiny, ragged spot on the bottom of the thick stage curtain. It was so minuscule that he almost missed it. The top of the bullet must have barely grazed it. Joe then looked at the back of the stage, yards behind the curtain, and saw it—a small hole in the wall.

He called a forensics tech who had just arrived over to take photos of both the curtain and the wall. Then they carefully dug a bullet, a thirty-caliber, out of the brick. It was arguably the most commonly used ammunition in the area, a favorite of deer hunters.

As Joe went back and stood in the spot where he had been standing when the shots were fired, he came to two conclusions—one, he was lucky he hadn't been shot, and two: this wasn't an arbitrary act. The shooter had had a target—possibly himself, or Pastor Kate. If it had been a random shooting or an attempted mass shooting, the shooter could have easily done more damage or hit easier targets. Instead, the shots had been fired into the same small area and the shooter stopped after only two shots.

Joe understood that, as an officer of the law, he had some enemies—but Pastor Kate? Why would anyone want to harm someone like her? He guessed the answer would have to wait. He was going home to be with Jodie, but he would begin investigating the answer the second he got there. In the meantime, deputies and troopers from the State Patrol and other law enforcement officers were on the hunt for the shooter, but so far, no luck.

Chapter 4

"Kate"

There was a very loud sound. Someone must have dropped something, or perhaps something fell. Kate remembered the tables of auction items and turned her head. Perhaps one of them had collapsed under the weight of some heavy prize. Earlier, she had noticed a lawnmower positioned on top of one of them, which had seemed quite precarious in her estimation.

Then she heard another loud bang. She felt a searing pain and something wet on her chest. She heard screams and shouting, then things went dark. She heard muffled voices and felt herself being lifted, but she couldn't open her eyes. Later she heard a beeping gadget of some sort and a siren, both of which were quite annoying, but she still couldn't seem to come to and tell someone to please shut them off.

Where had she been again? Why had she been there? Oh, yes, there was a dance. She should have stayed home. Why couldn't she open her eyes? Her mind just kept drifting in and out of darkness. People's voices kept coming and going and making little sense.

And then there was *his* voice. A voice from her past. If she could have moved, she would have pushed it away, or run away, or at least covered her ears. She hadn't thought of him since coming to Farmerton—not until earlier that day, when the roses had come. Roses—she remembered getting red roses. There was a card attached to them and it had terrified her. She should have told Joe about it. She should have told him about everything. She should call him, or ask someone else to call him, but then she remembered she couldn't seem to do anything.

Maybe she could try to open her mouth, but she felt someone put something over it and her nose. The annoying noises seemed to lessen, and Kate's mind drifted once more toward the voice.

January 1989

It was the first day of her very last semester of college. Don Henley's hit, *The End of the Innocence*, had recently been released and ruled the airways. Years later, Elizabeth Katherine Jones would remark it could have been her theme song for that year.

Elizabeth only had two required classes that semester, so she got to choose the others. For whatever reason, she decided to take a class that was cross-listed between the Sociology Department and the Law School, entitled The Sociology of Law. It sounded interesting and unique and might look impressive on her transcript if she ever chose to pursue a master's degree in social work, her major, in the future. Right now, she couldn't imagine more school. She could only think about being done with the endless amount of reading, papers, and blue-book final exams she'd taken over the past four years at the university.

Little did she know that her life would be forever

changed that afternoon when she sat down in the law school's large lecture hall. Being unfamiliar with the building, she was one of the final students to arrive, and found only a handful of seats unoccupied, all of which were in the front row. As if she didn't feel out of her league already, now she would have to sit right in front of the professor.

Elizabeth had felt uncomfortable and intimidated the moment she had passed through the doorway of the law building, with its heavy wood and brass doors. She had rushed past a huge library adorned with dark wood tables and Tiffany lamps, encompassed by endless floor-to-ceiling rows of books. She wondered if she really should have taken on the challenge of a class in a professional school, but it was too late now. She sheepishly slid into her seat just as the professor began speaking.

She hastily took out her notebook and began scribbling down every word the man said. At the end of the class, which had been interesting but extremely fast-paced, she finally looked up from her notes.

"Do you have stock in a pen company?"

She turned to her left, where the deep voice had come from. "Pardon?"

A young man smiled at her. He had perfect white teeth, and his thick, wavy blond hair was meticulously coiffed. He wore a long-sleeved, pale blue button-down shirt, which made his cornflower-blue eyes pop.

Elizabeth could barely speak. "I'm not sure I understand your question," she finally remarked softly.

"I just meant that if you keep taking so many detailed notes, you may want to consider purchasing stock in a pen company—and perhaps a paper company, too," he said, smiling even wider and leaning closer to her. She could smell the scent of his cologne. She didn't know the fragrance, but she found it intoxicating. She didn't know any other college students who wore cologne to class, but maybe it was common in law school.

It took everything she had to pull herself together to answer him. "I'll think about it," she finally said, and stood up to put on her coat. She had another class to get to in ten minutes on the other side of the large campus. She would barely make it in time, even without the chitchat.

He laughed lightly at her answer and helped her with her coat, which she found both charming and disarming.

"Thanks," she said quietly, stuffing her notebook into her backpack and then scurrying out of the row, which was now empty except for the two of them. He watched her as she left. At first, she didn't dare look back, but just as she reached the top of the lecture hall and exited, she turned her head. He was gone.

Two days later, when class reconvened, Elizabeth made sure to be one of the first students there. She planned to stay away from the front row, but, more than that, she hoped to avoid having to sit next to the handsome young man. She wondered what he would think if he knew how much time she had spent thinking about him over the past forty-eight hours—his eyes, his hair, his smile, even his cologne. To say he dominated her thoughts would be a huge understatement.

Elizabeth chose a seat in the center of the second-to-last row of the hall and did her best not to scan the room as it filled with students. A young woman sat down two seats away from her to her right. Then she felt someone sit down in the seat directly on her left. She didn't have to wonder who it was, as the scent of his cologne filled her senses. It was the same young man.

She tried to act nonchalant, but even though she was sitting down, her heart was pounding. Finally, she found the courage to look at him. He gave her one of his brilliant smiles and she was a goner. She was certain he would make a powerful lawyer in a courtroom with that grin of his, if that was the type of law he chose to practice. The professor began to speak, and she pulled herself away from the young man's gaze.

Elizabeth felt self-conscious the entire class time. She was trying to take fewer notes but also didn't want to miss anything important. She noticed the young man took very few notes, which made her feel silly and inadequate in comparison. She never should have taken this course.

Finally, the class was over, and she couldn't wait to get out of there. She was certain that this guy must have concluded that she had no business being in that class. And, truth be told, at that moment, she felt she was way out of her league in every way one could be.

That's why she was shocked when he helped her with her coat again, then simply asked, "Dinner tonight?"

Elizabeth looked around to see if he was indeed speaking to her. When she saw that it was just the two of them in the immediate area, she had to think fast. How could she get out of this situation? She knew if she went out with him, he would quickly discover she was not his type, and it would be a disaster. It was a Thursday, and she had no classes the next day, so she couldn't really use that as an excuse. She could say she had to study, which was weak, but believable. She opened her mouth to speak when he spoke again.

"Nothing too fancy, but if you have a dress, that would be best," he said, smiling again.

"Okay," she said quietly.

He introduced himself as Conrad. They exchanged phone numbers, and after securing her address, he told her he would pick her up at six-thirty.

Elizabeth went to her last class of the day, not hearing a word the professor said. Afterward, she walked the two-and-a-half miles home to the apartment she shared with her friend, Jacki, who had a lab until late. Elizabeth couldn't wait to tell her apartment mate what was going on, but first she needed to take a shower. Maybe then she would wake up from this dream.

An hour later, wrapped in a towel, she stood in front of her closet, gazing at the paltry selection inside. There was a black dress she wore for choir concerts. It wasn't too bad, she thought. She couldn't wait to be done with school and have a real job, not just the ten hours a week she spent as a project assistant for a professor. Hopefully, next year at this time she would have enough money to buy a new and better wardrobe. She pulled the garment off the hanger and held the black dress up to her image in the mirror. It would have to do.

Present Day – Before the Dance

Kate held the black dress in her hand as she prepared for the dance, her eyes stinging. It had reminded her of that night long ago, the one when she went on her first date with Conrad Kramer and her life was forever changed.

In those first days and weeks after they met, Elizabeth had been so utterly and completely enthralled by Conrad. He had been everything she was not. Conrad was from Chicago, a resident of the area referred to as the "Gold Coast." His parents were second-generation lawyers. The family had season tickets to musicals, plays, operas, and the ballet, were members of the Art Institute and the Field Museum, and were well-traveled. Conrad's sister, Katrina, was a graduate of Stanford University, and later the law school Conrad now attended. It was the family tradition. She was now an attorney with the firm their parents partnered.

Elizabeth Katherine, on the other hand, had grown up on the family farm. She helped with chores, knew how to drive a tractor, sang in the church and school choirs, and was a member of the local 4-H club. Her family rarely traveled, and Elizabeth hadn't flown in a plane until she was eighteen. It wasn't until college that she had gone to her first plays and musicals put on by music and theater majors. She thought they were magnificent. She could only imagine what it might be like to see a show in a big city like Chicago.

Tears had come to Kate's eyes as she put on the dress. She didn't wear too many clothes that weren't business suits of some sort—an occupational hazard of her years in law, and later in the church. She thought she had successfully left her past in the past—until the roses and card had arrived. She shouldn't have stayed in Farmerton for so long.

Chapter 5

Joe called the hospital and was informed that Pastor Kate was in surgery. A nurse promised to text him when she was out, since he was working the case and the pastor had no known family. The next hours would be critical, the nurse told him. Joe wasn't much of a praying man, but he sent up a little request for his pastor's recovery, knowing she would have appreciated it. Then he started making calls and exploring the internet.

Half an hour earlier, he had held Jodie tight until she fell asleep. It usually took a lot to rattle his wife, but she had never been quite the same since her abduction—she was just a bit leerier, a little more easily unnerved, than she had been before that haunting experience. Therapy with a counselor and many talks with Pastor Kate certainly helped, but Jodie would never quite be the same person again.

Joe checked into the church's social media presence online, the little there was of it. The pastor's name was listed, but there were no photos of her on the page. It did give an emergency number for the pastor, a landline number for the parsonage. Then Joe checked for social media accounts for Kate Roberts. A good number of faces showed up, but none of them matched the pastor's. Apparently, she had no desire to be on any type of social media platform, which he thought might not be such a bad thing these days.

He then looked up her name in the database. Again, there were other Kate Roberts, but none seemed to match the one he knew. That was strange. It was getting late, and Joe was exhausted. He thought he should probably try to get a bit of sleep, if that was even possible. His mind was racing. He wanted to be out looking for the shooter but knew that almost every law enforcement officer in the area was doing just that.

Joe felt a bit guilty, but he decided to stay home with his pregnant wife. He also knew he could be called upon at any time, especially if things went sideways with Pastor Kate. As he thought of the kind woman who was always taking care of others, he sent up one last prayer. Then Joe crept into their bedroom and laid down on the bed next to Jodie, fully dressed, just in case.

Several hours later, he received the message that the pastor was out of surgery. She would be put in the intensive care unit. The nurse mentioned that the next twenty-four hours would be critical. He looked over at Jodie and prayed that everything would be okay. He didn't think his wife could take another major loss in her life. She had already lost her one and only sibling, her brother, Jake, who had died in a car accident caused by an intoxicated driver. He knew that Jodie had grown quite fond of the pastor, and hoped all would end well, for everyone's sake. Then his heavy eyes closed, and Joe fell back to sleep.

Joe awakened to the sound of a flushing toilet in their ensuite bath, then listened to the slow footsteps of his sleepy, very pregnant wife. He felt Jodie climb back into bed and turned toward her.

"I'm sorry if we woke you up," she said gently, stroking the side of his face with her soft, warm hand.

Joe loved it whenever Jodie said "we" rather than "I." He gently laid his hand on Jodie's stomach. Lately, there had been a lot of kicking and turning going on and it seemed surreal. He couldn't quite fathom the idea of what it must be like to have another human being developing inside one's body, and was more intrigued every day. It was as if he was witnessing a miracle right before his eyes.

Even though Jodie woke up often during these late-pregnancy nights, it only took her moments to fall back asleep. Her eyes quickly closed, and her breathing slowed. As Jodie often mentioned, it was a lot of work growing another human being. Joe had no doubt that was true.

Joe, on the other hand, was now wide awake. He kept replaying the events at the dance over and over, and shuddered at the thought that Jodie could have been right next to Pastor Kate if she hadn't had to use the restroom, and she—and the baby—could have been wounded, or worse.

Joe kept going back to his question about why the shooter had only shot two bullets with a deer rifle, rather than shooting into the mass of people with a more efficient automatic rifle. Again, he thought it seemed more like a targeted shooting, but why the pastor, and why in such a public place?

Joe sat up and swung his feet to the floor, then quietly tiptoed out of the room, grabbing his laptop on the way out. He decided to go to the dining room rather than to the small office downstairs. It was warmer in the dining room, and he could spread out at the large oak table. He did much of his best thinking at the table. Before opening his computer, he checked in with the officer in charge to see if there had been any new developments in the case, and then with the hospital as to the pastor's condition.

There was more information about the getaway vehicle. The black SUV had been found with no fingerprints other than those of the previous owners at a crossroads about five miles out of town. The car had been registered to a person in southeastern Wisconsin, who had sold it for cash to another person several months before. He had signed over the title, and the buyer, a young woman, had been on her way with barely a word. They took down the description of this person, as much as the man could remember from that time. He had just been happy to unload his "gas guzzler" quickly and without any hassle. He didn't really pay much attention to anything other than making sure to count the stack of twenty-dollar bills the person had used to buy it.

Therefore, the identity and whereabouts of the shooter remained a mystery. They supposed the person might have come from southeastern Wisconsin, where the vehicle had been purchased, but couldn't be sure of that. And as to what happened after the person abandoned the vehicle, they could only guess that someone picked them up and gave them a ride. But who? And which way had they gone?

As for Pastor Kate, she would be in intensive care for an undetermined amount of time. She was currently intubated, also for an indefinite time. Upon operating, the surgeon had found her wound more extensive than expected. There was a little better than sixty-percent chance of full recovery—not great, but not terrible when dealing with a "GSW," a gunshot wound. Meanwhile, the hospital was asking if anyone had any information about the pastor's family, as they were hitting a dead-end in that department.

Joe thought about Pastor Kate lying in a hospital bed all alone, with no one at her side. He knew that she always visited people who were in the hospital, even when it meant driving over an hour each way at times. He was determined he would make it there sometime during the day, but he needed to help find the shooter, track down some of the pastor's family, and figure out why any of this had happened. He decided that at the earliest reasonable time, he would begin by calling the church secretary, Margaret Miller, and see what information she had about Pastor Kate. If anyone knew, or could find out, it would be her.

The next morning, Margaret Miller pulled a file from an old metal filing cabinet in the church office.

"This is all I have on the pastor," she said.

Joe opened the thin file. In it, he found the pastor's employment history, which listed the interim calls she had taken over the past almost twenty years, each with the name and phone number of a reference. It also had her current address at the parsonage, her last-known address prior to her work in Farmerton, her personal cell phone number, and her church retirement account number, as St. John's regularly made payments to it. There was no other information, unfortunately.

"That's all there is?" Joe asked disappointedly.

"I'm afraid so. We don't require emergency contact information—perhaps that is something we will have to consider in the future. I'll have to mention it to the church council president—but not right now. He is in an absolute panic about tomorrow, as he will be filling in for Pastor Kate at worship. Hopefully, he can find a pastor to fill in for future weeks, until Pastor Kate can return. She should be able to return, shouldn't she?"

"I hope so," was all Joe could say.

"What a day yesterday was," Margaret said. "First, the fainting spell—then the shooting!"

"Yes. What exactly happened yesterday when the pastor passed out?"

"Well, I had just handed her a bouquet of beautiful red roses that had been delivered to the office for her. She took the flowers, then read the little card that came with them, and then down she went!"

"What was on the card? Do you know who the flowers were from?"

"I have no idea. All I know is that they came from Blooms and Baskets, but I have no idea who sent them. The flowers and the note were no longer here when I opened the office this morning."

"Do you mind if I look around?"

"Go right ahead, Sergeant."

Joe looked around the pastor's office first. There was no sign of flowers anywhere. He even checked the trash can near Margaret's desk, but there was nothing there.

"Are there any other trash cans around here?"

"Not in the office area. There are some in the Sunday School rooms and in the narthex for coffee hour, and then there's the dumpster outside."

Joe checked the other receptacles, but no flowers. He really didn't want to go back out into the cold, but decided he had to be thorough. At least it was a small dumpster, and if something was thrown away the day before, it shouldn't be hard to find.

He lifted the heavy lid, which creaked in the cold. He turned on the flashlight on his phone for better lighting and surveyed the contents of the dumpster. It wasn't too nasty, not like he was sure it would be after the remnants of Sunday refreshments the next morning.

And there they were. A bouquet of red roses, still in their clear wrapper, right on top. Of course, they were just out of his reach, so he had to crawl over the side of the heavy metal bin and get inside to retrieve them. He put on gloves, then made his way into the container.

The roses had turned a darker red and were black around the edges, having frozen overnight, but they were intact. There was no note on them, however, so he kept looking. He turned and noticed a small, crumpled envelope. He grabbed it and threw it and the flowers out of the bin, then hoisted himself out of the dumpster. It had been much easier getting in than it was getting out.

Joe put the roses and card in his cruiser, not wanting Margaret to know what he had found and gossip to ensue. He carefully opened the card and read the single word on it—B-I-T...! Joe gasped. Who would call Pastor Kate such a word? And why?

Joe dropped the note and the roses into an evidence bag, then took off the gloves and went back inside to talk to Margaret.

"Is there any chance I can get into the parsonage and look around?" Joe asked the secretary.

"I'll call the council president, and he should be able to let you in."

The council president told Margaret he would meet Joe at the pastor's home in fifteen minutes.

The church president appeared frazzled and worried as he and Joe walked up the frosty steps and into the parsonage.

"I feel like I'm being tested," the gentleman told Joe. "I agreed to serve a three-year term, just when Pastor Kate came on board. I was sure we were past the craziness that occurred with the murders, but then there was that awful business with your wife, and now this."

Joe understood how the man felt. He still couldn't believe all that had transpired in their tiny community in the past five years. He never could have imagined such hardships as murders and a kidnapping happening in the quiet town he had grown up in.

The council president went home, telling Joe to lock the front door when he left. Joe put a new pair of gloves on and started to search the downstairs, even though he had no idea what he was looking for exactly. He went upstairs and looked in the bedrooms. There were three rooms—one of which the pastor used as a study, the other as a guest room, and then the main bedroom. He noticed the closet door was open. He looked inside, but there was nothing that seemed out of the ordinary. There were several business suits, clerical shirts of many colors, a few pairs of shoes, purses of various sizes, and an old but expensive-looking leather briefcase on the top shelf.

He turned and noticed a small backpack, the one the pastor often used, sitting on top of the dresser. He remembered that she had carried a small clutch purse with her at the event, which had been sent with her to the hospital. Joe felt uncomfortable doing it, but he decided to look inside the pack. He found her wallet, which was minus her driver's license, looking for any clues to family, but there were none.

Joe looked around the house one more time. What struck him was the lack of photos anywhere, not even on her dresser. He thought about his own home, adorned with photos of family and friends on walls, dresser tops, and fireplace mantels. Feeling disappointed and frustrated, he locked up and went back to his cruiser.

Joe sat for a moment, staring at the evidence bag. He wasn't sure it was related to the shooting, but until it was ruled out, he was keeping it. Joe decided his next stop should be Blooms and Baskets. And as he started the engine, he thought out loud, "What in the world is going on, Pastor Kate?"

Blooms and Baskets was a small but popular shop on the main street of a nearby town. Today it was relatively quiet, the display cases picked over after the Valentine's Day rush. The owner was working, as she had given everyone but one delivery person the day off after the marathon the previous day. Of course, there were still a few people celebrating the day after Valentine's Day, so she stayed open for those customers.

Joe asked the owner if she could determine who had purchased the roses that were delivered to Pastor Kate at St. John's Church the day before. She nodded and started checking her computer.

"The person must have used cash, as there is no credit card information for a rose transaction being delivered to that address this past week."

Joe was disappointed. "Did you take the order?" he asked.

"No, it was one of my employees. Would you like his name and phone number?"

"Yes, that would be helpful," Joe replied.

Joe knew it was a long shot, but perhaps the salesperson remembered what the person looked like. After several calls going to voicemail, he finally spoke with the young man, but he may as well not have, as the clerk couldn't remember the buyer very well. He thought it might have been a younger woman, but he wasn't certain. The worker, who sounded like he had just crawled out of bed, had taken hundreds of orders earlier that week, and they were all blending together in his mind.

Once more, Joe felt frustrated as he climbed into his cruiser. He checked in with the department to see if there were any other leads in the case, or if anyone had reached Pastor Kate's family, to which the answer was a resounding "no." Then he called Jodie.

"Hi, hon," he said to his wife. "How are you doing?"

"I'm very tired today, so I'm just going to lay low," she said wearily.

Joe didn't like the sound of her voice. "I had been thinking about checking on Pastor Kate, but maybe I should stay home with you."

"Don't you dare not see Pastor Kate on my account. I'll be fine. Please see her and apologize for me not being there."

"There's nothing to apologize about, Jodie. Pastor Kate

would be the first person to tell you that."

"I know she would, but just let her know I'm there in spirit—and hold her hand for me," Jodie said, her voice beginning to break.

"I will, sweetheart."

Joe wanted to go home and hold his wife, but he knew he should get to Madison as soon as possible, as there was bad weather heading their way in the next twenty-four hours. The good news was that the temperatures would be warmer for the next few days. The bad news was the precipitation the change would bring.

Joe started the engine and his phone rang, announcing some more unwanted news.

"Joe," the sheriff said, "I wanted to tell you first off because I know you are a friend of hers. I just heard that Sissy Roth is in St. Mary's Hospital in Madison. It appears she may have suffered a heart attack. They are doing tests as we speak."

Joe's head swam. No wonder Sissy had seemed so tired the day before; she was sick. Now two people he cared about were in a hospital in Madison. He called Jodie to tell her of his plans. He would check on the pastor first, and then go see Sissy on his way out of the city. The weekend was turning from a bad dream into a nightmare.

Chapter 6

Joe usually loved driving into Madison. It was one of his and Jodie's favorite places to go for a special dinner, a show, a sporting event, or some other type of fun. But today his destinations were the exact opposite of fun.

Joe had come to despise hospitals ever since his father's too-early death, and he wanted to leave the second he stepped foot in the intensive care unit. A kind nurse showed him to the pastor's room and pulled a chair next to the hospital bed for him. He sat down and the nurse told him not to stay too long, then left to check on other patients.

Joe watched Pastor Kate's chest methodically rise and fall with every noisy, machine-assisted breath. Another machine emitted quiet sounds as it recorded her heartbeat, blood pressure, and oxygen levels, and an IV sent essential fluids and medications to her body. He was really struggling with seeing her like this, more than he would have ever imagined. Joe was tempted to bolt for the door but willed himself to stay in the chair next to her bed.

He remembered being told people could hear you speak, even if they were unconscious, so Joe told the pastor all the updates he had at that point about her surgery and the shooting, leaving out the part about how upset Jodie was, as well as the discovery of the roses and note. He didn't want to mention anything that might upset

Pastor Kate and impede her recovery. He talked to the pastor as if she could answer, wondering how something like this could have happened in Farmerton. It made him feel better to unload on her, even if she couldn't respond, and realized what a sounding board she had become for not only Jodie, but for himself.

He felt better when he finished his spiel, then remembered what Jodie had asked him to do. Joe looked around. Seeing there was no one at the desk behind the large glass window, he took the pastor's hand and lightly squeezed it. "This is from Jodie, Pastor. And this is from me," he said, squeezing it once more. "I'm going to get to the bottom of this. I promise," he said, finding himself becoming emotional. That was Joe's cue to be on his way.

There were more noisy machines in Sissy's room, but at least she was conscious and could talk. Her husband, Jon, had driven her to the hospital that morning after she could barely get out of a chair at home. Afraid of the expense of an ambulance ride, Jon had loaded Sissy into his pickup truck and drove her to the hospital in Madison instead. It was a good thing that he had, as bloodwork showed she had suffered a heart attack. She already had completed some tests, and was scheduled for more later that afternoon.

Sissy's husband, who usually tried to act tough, was at her side and driving her crazy with his hypervigilance of her every movement. Finally, she convinced him to go to the cafeteria now that Joe was there, as Jon hadn't eaten yet that day because of the emergency. He reluctantly gave in.

"Thank goodness you came, Joe," Sissy said after her

husband left the room. "Jon means well, but he is going to give me another heart attack if he doesn't leave me alone. How did you find out?"

Joe told her that the sheriff—who had heard the news from a friend of Jon's at the gas station—had told him because he knew Joe and Sissy were friends.

"I'm glad he told you. And I'm glad you're my friend, Joe. I need a friend right now," Sissy said, her eyes filling with tears.

"It will be okay, Sissy, they can do a lot to fix hearts these days..." Joe started to say when Sissy interrupted him.

"It's not my heart I'm worried about," she said, turning her head away from him and staring toward the window. "I have a confession to make," she said weakly.

Joe wasn't expecting to hear something like this and was at a loss for words momentarily. He tried to remember how his and Jodie's counselor, and Pastor Kate, would handle tough moments like this.

So, he quietly said, "Go on."

Sissy slowly turned back to him, her eyes red and watery. "I've gotten myself into a real pickle, Joe, and I don't know how to get out." She sniffed, and Joe handed her a small, flat box of tissues that was on the tray table next to her bed.

Sissy took a tissue, blew her nose, and continued. "It all started at 'the boat.'"

"The boat" needed little explanation to many in the tri-state area. It referred to a popular gambling casino in Dubuque.

"I went with some friends one night a few months ago and won a good chunk of money. It was so much fun. So,

I went back again—and again—and again, except I never won—I only lost. Now, all my credit cards are maxed out, and I'm afraid..." Sissy's voice broke again. "I'm afraid if I can't get out of this, I'm going to lose my shop—and I love my shop. It's the best thing in my life."

Joe loved Sissy's shop, too, and so did everyone in Farmerton, even those who didn't frequent the salon. Sissy's Scissors always helped sponsor community events, and supported clubs and schools, in addition to being a long-enduring business on Main Street. It was more than just a beauty salon; it was an institution—a place where people came not only for good haircuts, but for good conversation. Joe couldn't imagine Sissy's Scissors going under.

Joe wasn't sure how to respond to this surprising news, but for the second time in a day, he found himself holding someone's hand. "Does anyone else know?" he asked gently.

"You're the only one, Joe."

"I know it will be difficult, Sissy, but I think you're going to have to tell Jon—and soon."

"I know. I wanted to, but I just couldn't tell him. His entire family has been so proud of us, that we seem to be doing well compared to others in his family, and now this. I've never been so irresponsible in my life. I just don't know what came over me. Now, I worry about it all day long and can't sleep nights. Then this past week—with it being so crazy busy at work—I think my heart just couldn't handle it anymore."

"It will be tough to tell Jon, but I'm sure you can find a way out of this. It's not worth risking your health, Sissy. Jon loves you—I can tell that. You'll get through this—together."

"You're right, Joe. I'll tell him, but I'm not looking forward to it," she said, with a tiny, forced laugh.

"If you were, I'd be really worried about you, Sissy, even more than I was the first time you threw that hot pink cape around my neck and started snipping away."

That made Sissy laugh, for real this time. "You looked so scared," she said, remembering the day Joe had come in for a haircut while hoping to learn something about a local murder case.

"I'd never been to a beauty salon before. In fact, you were only the second female to ever cut my hair. The other was my sister, when she was eight and I was five, and that didn't go very well," Joe remarked.

That made them both laugh, and that was the way Jon found them when he returned from a quick lunch, carrying a carnation in a small, clear vase he had bought at the gift shop downstairs. Sissy looked shocked at the gift, as Jon rarely spent money on non-essentials.

"I've got to get back to my wife," Joe said. "Sissy, you get well now. You've got this," he said.

"You give that sweetie of yours a big hug, Joe. She's a lucky lady," Sissy said.

"I'm the lucky one," Joe said, meaning it, and headed out the door.

When Joe got off the elevator on the ground floor, he caught a whiff of some gourmet coffee brewing down the hall at a small bistro. He stopped for a cup and a sandwich to go and headed to his car. He felt like he was in a dream again, not unlike when Farmerton was dealing with murders and Jodie's kidnapping. He guessed life was just full of all kinds of surprises, and he knew he would probably discover more after he got home to his computer.

He wasn't wrong.

Chapter 7

Kate still couldn't open her eyes or speak. She had heard Joe Zimmerman talking to her earlier, but she couldn't answer him. She couldn't tell him about the note, about the entire situation. He had told her that when she woke up, he had some questions for her, so maybe he already found it. But that didn't help him much. He had no idea who he might be dealing with—and, for that matter, she wasn't sure *she* knew who they were dealing with, either. It could be any one of a number of people, although the first one who came to mind was her "ex." She just couldn't wake up, though, and soon she drifted back off.

January 1989

Elizabeth stood outside her six-unit apartment building for only a moment before a silver BMW sports car zipped into the small parking lot in front of her building. The passenger window rolled down and she saw the smiling face of Conrad, who was stretched across the front seat to greet her.

"Let's go," he said, and she opened the car door quickly and hopped in on the frigid evening.

She had barely buckled up when Conrad zoomed out of the parking lot, the back end of the car fishtailing a bit in the snow and ice, but it didn't seem to faze him at all. His calmness helped make her feel safe somehow, even though she knew her parents would not approve of the way Conrad was driving with their daughter in the car.

Conrad's cologne smelled even better than Elizabeth remembered, and she felt flushed as he turned up the music. The vehicle had an outstanding sound system, of course. They were heading toward downtown, and Elizabeth was excited when they pulled into the private parking lot behind a restaurant known for its top-quality steaks. She had heard of the place, but she never would have chosen such an expensive spot. Elizabeth hoped she had enough money in her purse in case they shared the bill. While Conrad had been the one to ask her to dinner, she didn't want to assume anything at this point in their relationship, if one could even call what they had a relationship.

The evening had been magical. Tables with white linens and candlelight, wine brought to the table and taste-tested by her date, who also ordered for them. She thought she was either dreaming or had somehow been transported into one of the romantic movies she and her girlfriends enjoyed on many Friday nights.

Conrad was a gentleman all evening. He had even managed to compliment her on her dress, although she could tell he was unimpressed. That perception was solidified that weekend when he suggested they go shopping. He said he needed some dress shirts, but he encouraged her to try on some dresses at a store in an upscale mall in town.

She was reluctant, as she mentioned that clothes shopping was not in her budget at the time. But he told her to do it—just for fun. He had impeccable taste, seeming to know just what would look flattering on her. Elizabeth had never worn such elegant clothing and knew there was no way she was going to purchase them, as they cost more than her textbooks had for the semester.

Elizabeth handed the clothes back to the clerk after dressing in her own clothes, but Conrad told the clerk that he would take the dresses, too, along with the shirts he had chosen. They then stopped at the jewelry counter, as he mentioned one must accessorize when one has dresses like those.

Elizabeth felt uncomfortable about the entire situation, but Conrad was a difficult person to say no to, so she let him spoil her. If spoiling had been all there was to it, it wouldn't have been a problem at all, but years later she had realized that that weekend had been only the beginning of his manipulative and controlling behavior—over every aspect of her life.

Yet, she couldn't seem to stop the way she felt about him. He took her out for dinner at a French restaurant after shopping, ordering for them once more—this time in French. He was so romantic. He was so handsome. And, apparently, so wealthy.

Everything about him was intoxicating, and that's how Elizabeth found herself staying the night at his apartment, something she had never done before on just a second date. And by the time she went home the following day, after he had made her a perfect omelet for breakfast, she announced to her roommate, Jacki, that she was in love, and someday she was going to marry Conrad Kramer.

Chapter 8

Joe pulled out of the hospital parking ramp, looking both ways before he turned. Once on the quiet street behind the hospital, he took a sip of the delicious coffee and was just going to take a bite of his sandwich when his cell phone rang. It was his friend, Simon.

"What's up, Simon?"

There was a pause on Simon's end, then he spoke quietly. "We heard from the adoption agency."

"Already?" Joe asked.

"They said they would do their best, but it's doubtful we will be candidates for adoption because of my alcoholism, even if I'm in recovery."

"Gee, that's rough, Simon," Joe said. "Did they read my recommendation?"

"Yes, and thank you again," he said, the disappointment mounting in his voice. "I guess we'll never be parents."

"I've learned to never say never, Simon. Hang in there," Joe said.

"I'll try," Simon said unconvincingly. "Hey, I've got to go, Joe, but I just wanted to keep you up to date."

"I appreciate it, Simon. Let me know if there's anything else I can do to help."

"I will. Take care, Joe," Simon said and hung up.

Joe felt so bad for Simon and Sally. There had to be

another answer for them, but he just didn't know what it was yet. Pastor Kate might have some ideas, but of course, she was unable to share any of her expertise right now.

Joe thought about what it must be like for the pastor on a regular basis. Today he felt like he was getting a little taste of what she did every day. There were always people experiencing some sort of emergency, heartache, or other problem, and often without warning. It wasn't unlike being a police officer, but at least he had the rest of the department and other agencies in the area for backup. It didn't seem like Pastor Kate had any of those, but maybe the other pastors in the area helped each other. He sure hoped there was some kind of support system for them.

Joe stopped at one of their favorite bakeries on the way home and bought some fresh-baked wholegrain bread to take home to Jodie. It would make for some great grilled cheese sandwiches. He thought he could make those for Jodie that night for dinner, along with some tomato soup. They fell into the category of comfort food, and they, along with everyone in Farmerton, needed comfort right now.

Joe turned on the radio to listen to some music and hear the latest weather forecast. It had been warmer when he came out of the hospital than when he had arrived. He was certain they were going to get a good dose of snow that night. He couldn't wait to get home, and especially to his beloved Jodie. And, of course, the baby. The thought of that made him smile.

Jodie was elated to see Joe and threw her arms around him the second he walked through the door. The day had seemed endless without him. All there was to do was think about Pastor Kate and Sissy in the hospital, and Joe getting home before the big storm came in that night. And on top of it, she had felt ridiculously tired, a bit nauseous, and had spent a significant time in the bathroom the entire time Joe was gone. She was worried she might be coming down with the flu on top of everything else that was going on.

Joe and Jodie sat next to each other on the couch, as the wooden chairs at the dining table felt hard to Jodie these days. Joe filled Jodie in on all the things that had happened that day, except for Sissy's gambling and financial troubles. The next time he talked to Sissy he would ask her permission to share the information with his wife, but he felt it should just be between them for the time being. Besides, Jodie didn't need any more concerns on her plate right now. Taking care of herself and the baby was the number-one priority, and since she wasn't feeling all that great, it seemed best to leave out some of the details for now.

"I'm just glad you are home now," she said. "And they said they would let you know when Pastor Kate is awake?"

"They said they certainly would, especially since they can't find any family for her. I'm going to do some digging about that after dinner, but right now, I'm going to make supper, if you're up to it."

"It sounds wonderful, Joe. You are so kind," she said and kissed him softly on the lips.

"Don't start that, or I'll never get anything done. I'm already behind on my weekend plans. I was supposed to get that crib put together today. It will have to wait until tomorrow."

"It will still be there," she said. "Besides, we've got

time," Jodie said, knowing there were still weeks until their due date.

Joe made the sandwiches and soup, deciding that the stop at the bakery had indeed been worthwhile. The two ate heartily, and for Jodie, it was the first food that had any real appeal all day. After they finished eating, even though it was only eight o'clock, Jodie said she was going to lie down. She was still super tired. They kissed good-night and Joe headed to his office with his laptop.

"So, what's your story, Pastor Kate?" he asked himself.

He searched repeatedly using detailed information for a Kate Roberts, but still no luck. He went into the archives of the seminary she had attended in California and looked for the graduation classes around the time he had noted she graduated. There was her photo, with just her name.

He searched for emails with her name, and the only one he found was from her seminary days. It seemed so strange for someone not to have an email address. On the church's social media page, it only gave the church email, which he assumed the pastor accessed regularly. It was as if she hadn't existed before her seminary days, and there was little to learn about her since. Maybe that had something to do with the person who had written that nasty note to her, but Joe had no idea where to start on that.

He just couldn't imagine the pastor having that kind of enemy, and if he hadn't seen it for himself, he still wouldn't have believed it. But he now knew—there was someone out there who "had it in" for his pastor, and he was going to find out who it was, no matter what it took.

Chapter 9

Huge, wet flakes of snow began their assault around nine o'clock that evening. The forecast was changing from minute to minute, but they were still calling for up to twelve inches of snow. The church council president called the executive members of the council, and together they decided to cancel the church service for the next morning. Closures were beginning to pop up on the area television stations, and weather forecasters on the news stations told their audiences that anyone who didn't absolutely have to go out should not go out.

The council president tried hard not to sound happy on the phone, but he was inwardly elated and, even more so, relieved that there would be no service the next morning. Now he could stop trying to come up with some sort of message. No longer would he have to field a million questions about the pastor for which he had no answers. Instead, he sent out a group email to the church members and called the members who didn't have internet service. Luckily, there were not many of those anymore.

At the last minute, the president thought about the farmer from the area, Clifford Boyd, who had been coming to church services lately. He decided to call him and let him know about the cancellation. Luckily, Clifford still had a landline, as many farmers in the area did, and he found his number in an old phone book he kept in his desk drawer.

Clifford had been heading to bed when the council president called. After he put the wall phone receiver back in place, he sat at his small kitchen table. It was the same table he'd sat at for meals his entire life. He stared blankly at the wall for a few minutes, then came out of his trance-like state.

Clifford didn't really care that the church service had been called off, as he had not been planning to attend this week—or any week—ever again. He had experienced bitterness all week long.

Last Sunday, he had chosen a dozen of his best and freshest eggs to give to Pastor Kate. She was the reason he had been going to the church services lately. Several months earlier, Clifford's uncle, with whom he had been exceptionally close, had passed away. His uncle always said he wanted a religious funeral service, even though he hadn't gone to church in many years. So, when his uncle died, Clifford called a fair number of clergy members in the area, asking if they would preside at his uncle's funeral. Pastor Kate was the only one who had been willing to do the service.

Pastor Kate had treated Clifford's extended family like she would anyone who had lost a loved one. She had interviewed Clifford and his cousins about what kind of man his uncle had been, and gave the nicest sermon about him. It felt like the pastor had known his uncle for years, rather than never having met him at all.

The pastor had even let the family use the church basement for a potluck lunch after the burial. She had been so kind and always wore a smile on her face. But, most importantly to Clifford, she treated him like he was a normal person, which wasn't always the way he had been treated in his life. While Clifford was cognitively sound, he didn't always come across that way to other people. He was painfully shy and awkward, especially when he dealt with females. In social situations, he appeared to others as different—odd. He had heard one of his classmates' mothers call him an "odd duck" once when they were in elementary school—in front of some of his classmates. After that day, the children's nickname for him was "Ducky," which he loathed. What little self-esteem he may have once had left him that day, and never returned.

In high school, he skipped the dances and never participated in sports, even though he was one of the fastest runners in gym class. He despised reading out loud in class, and almost didn't pass English when he had to stand up in front of the class and give a speech, even though it was about farming—something he loved and knew well.

The only people he could easily talk to had been his parents and his uncle. Even his cousins made him feel self-conscious and thought he was strange. So, it wasn't hard to understand why Clifford thought of himself as someone no girl would want to date. There was a moment in high school when he thought he might have a chance, however. A new girl had moved to town. Her name was Carrie Anne, a petite girl with silky, long red hair. She was kind to him at first, then gave into peer pressure and was the same as the rest of his classmates. Since then, he'd pretty much given up on the thought of a relationship with anyone special.

His parents and uncle were gone now, and he found himself a sixty-year-old man living alone, who fully expected that would be his lot in life. Until he met the pastor. For whatever reason, he had let himself believe his luck may have turned. She had been kind to him and his family, and he didn't feel as nervous around her as he usually did around women.

Thus, one Sunday morning, he had decided he would go to her church, just to see her kind and smiling face once more. He'd gone back almost every week since. Last week, he felt so positive about things that he mustered the courage to bring the pastor a gift, but that had really backfired on him.

He had handed the pastor the carton of eggs, and she took them from him hesitantly. She thanked him, but then ruined it. She mentioned that she really wasn't supposed to take gifts from anyone, but she would make an exception "this one time." She said it in a kind voice, but all Clifford heard was another rejection.

Kate had felt bad saying that to Clifford, but after a recent mandatory clergy ethics training course—and some past negative experiences—she had been trying to avoid taking personal gifts. In one of the first churches she served, a man had misread her feelings for him after she had accepted several gifts from him. In another church, a woman had thought she could persuade Pastor Kate to make the changes she wanted at the church after the woman had gifted her a beautiful quilt she had made.

Clifford had pretended it hadn't bothered him when the pastor told him this was a one-time thing, but it didn't sit well with him at all. He sat in his truck after he walked out of the church and stewed about it for half an hour after the service. All the other parishioners had gone home, and he was still sitting there. Clifford looked around. It was just his truck and the pastor's car in the lot.

He didn't know what had possessed him, but Clifford

opened his glove compartment, jumped out of his truck with a tire gauge in hand, and, seeing no one nearby, let the air out of a tire on the driver's side of Pastor Kate's car. Then he sped off in his truck.

He had often felt like doing something mean to those who disappointed him in his past but hadn't had the courage. Years of pent-up rage had surfaced and started to overflow, and it needed to come out in some way.

All week long, Clifford had experienced a mixture of feelings. One minute he felt pangs of guilt. He had even thought about telling the pastor what he had done and apologizing. The next moment, he felt no remorse at all, only vindication. He was still waffling between emotions on this night, despite what had transpired the night before at the dance. The pastor had been shot and was in the hospital, fighting for her life. It made him feel bad at first, but then he thought perhaps Pastor Kate had gotten exactly what she deserved.

Chapter 10

Joe was so immersed in his computer search that he didn't even notice just how bad the weather had gotten until a notification pinged on his phone about the church service cancellation email. He felt bad admitting it, but after the little sleep he'd gotten the night before, and the emotional hospital visits during the day, he would be happy to stay home the next day. He could put the crib together, then watch the Super Bowl that evening, even though he wasn't particularly a fan of either team in the game this year. He would get back to Madison when he was on duty Monday, after the snowplows had done their work.

Joe turned back to the computer screen. He was absolutely mystified by the sparse information about Pastor Kate Roberts, so he started doing a deeper background check. He finally found a Kate Kristina Roberts who had lived in California years before. He knew the pastor had gone to seminary in California, so he thought perhaps that was her. Before that time, there was no information for anyone with that name, and there were no relatives listed. Joe dug deeper and finally found an association. Kate Kristina Roberts' name was listed with someone formerly known as Elizabeth Katherine Kramer and, prior to that, Elizabeth Katherine Jones. The latter had lived in numerous locales, first in Iowa, then Illinois, later the East Coast, and finally the West Coast of the United States.

Joe's eyes were getting blurry. He had to get some sleep.

He would check out this "Kate" business in the morning. He was exhausted after the long day of driving and visits, followed by hours staring at a computer screen. He decided to call it a night and headed to the bedroom.

Joe crept into bed, not even bothering to brush his teeth. He didn't want to wake up Jodie. She was up a few times a night to use the restroom lately, and he didn't need to disturb her sleep any more than her bladder already did. He gazed at his wife for a moment. He had never known such love before meeting her. He mouthed the words "I love you," then fell sound asleep.

Chapter 11

The room was filled with muffled voices she did not recognize. Kate had heard Joe Zimmerman's voice earlier, but it felt like forever ago. Joe and his wife, Jodie, were two of her favorite people, even though she knew she shouldn't have "favorite people." She had learned over the years not to get too attached to anyone she served, under any circumstance. It was hard on her spirit, knowing she would only have to leave them behind in the future. Part of that was due to the nature of her work as an interim. The other part was self-imposed. Over the years, she had left so many people behind. She was particularly not looking forward to the time when she would leave behind Joe and Jodie, and many other good people at St. John's.

The voices stopped and it was quiet again, except for a breathy, rhythmic sound. She was curious about it, but she couldn't seem to wake up, and she couldn't speak as something was in her throat. She thought she heard one of the people telling her that things would be better soon, but she couldn't be sure. She was so sleepy, and something was hurting her midsection. Kate felt like she was in a never-ending dream, and eventually she drifted back to where her thoughts had left off. It was Valentine's Day, a day she often wished had never existed.

Valentine's Day, 1989

Six weeks. Six weeks of Conrad Kramer. Six weeks of living in an intense love haze. Elizabeth spent almost every waking moment with Conrad, and when they weren't together, he dominated her thoughts and feelings. His romantic gestures. The incredible way he made her feel, especially when they made love. She had never known she could feel that way, physically or emotionally. Even a simple glance from him could make her melt. She couldn't get him out of her mind or heart. Elizabeth was completely smitten, as her mother would have said.

Considering all these feelings, Elizabeth was amazed she could keep up with all her coursework. However, the opposite was happening. She was doing better than ever in school. Elizabeth was motivated by Conrad, who was a brilliant student. He had also convinced her she was smart enough to go to law school. He paid for her to take the LSAT, the law school admission test that would be given at the end of the current month, and to apply for law school before the deadline in mid-March. They studied in the law library each evening, and then Conrad quizzed her on sample test questions, for which he seemed to know every answer. Elizabeth greatly admired his genius, along with all of his other fine qualities.

But tonight, they were taking a break from their normal weeknight routine. It was Valentine's Day. Elizabeth used to scoff at all the hoopla surrounding this day until she fell in love with Conrad. Tonight, they were going to celebrate this day devoted to love.

Conrad picked out the dress she should wear, as he

had informed her the evening was going to be special. Elizabeth thought every day with Conrad was special, but he could call it whatever he wanted, and she wouldn't argue. She pulled the garment out of the closet and got dressed, her heart full.

The city lights sparkled below. They were seated in a rooftop restaurant downtown. She had thought the steak house she and Conrad had gone to on their first date had been amazing, but this place was in another league. Now she understood why Conrad had insisted she wear one of her new outfits. He was just looking out for her.

Conrad's bright blue eyes twinkled that evening, even more than usual, and his gaze penetrated Elizabeth's very being. How could she love someone so much? How could she ever live without this person? Even when she was with him, she felt she was never close enough to him.

At the end of their meal, a flaming chocolate ball dessert arrived at their table. It was almost too pretty to eat, but Conrad insisted she try a bit. The dark chocolate melted as the server slowly poured hot espresso over it, revealing chunks of vanilla ice cream inside. She ate a bite, then noticed something else in her dessert. It was a small box. She surmised it was there to keep the ice cream from melting or something. She pushed the plate away when she had eaten the ice cream, so full she almost felt ill.

"You might want to open that before you send it back to the kitchen," Conrad said.

"Open what?"

"That box."

She pulled the plate back, took the small container from it carefully, and opened it. There was a small velvet box inside. Conrad was giving her jewelry! She was excited, but completely unprepared for what happened next. As she opened the box, she noticed Conrad suddenly at her side, on one knee. Inside the satin-lined box there was a sparkling diamond ring.

"Marry me, Elizabeth Katherine Jones."

Elizabeth felt lightheaded. Was Conrad really proposing to her? Did he really feel about her the way she felt about him? Tears formed in her eyes. She never felt before, or ever again, the way she felt that night.

"I would love to marry you, Conrad Christian Kramer."

They stood and kissed, the rest of the world disappearing. When they came back to reality, the waiter, along with people at the nearby tables, were nodding approvingly and congratulating them. They did make a stunning couple. The waiter snapped a photo after Conrad instructed him as to how to operate his brand-new Canon EOS-1 single-lens reflex camera to capture the special moment. It was a moment Elizabeth would never forget.

They could hardly keep their hands off one another all the way back to Conrad's apartment. Wisely, Kate had started keeping a clean change of clothes at Conrad's, as she seemed to be there more often than at her own apartment.

She thought their time together had been wonderful before, but their passion after their engagement rose to a new level. In the morning, Elizabeth looked at the ring on her finger to make sure it hadn't been a dream, then looked at Conrad, who was watching her intently. They looked into one another's eyes.

"Hello, future Mrs. Kramer," Conrad said, gently reaching for her left hand and kissing it.

"Hello right back at you, Mr. Kramer."

They were utterly consumed with each other. It felt like no one could stand between them now. No one—except, perhaps, their parents.

Even though the Jones and Kramer families were as different as night and day, with one set living in rural northwest Iowa and the other in Chicago, their basic responses to their children's engagement had been quite similar.

"What were you thinking?" Conrad's father had asked loudly, a vein in his temple throbbing in anger. "Who is this girl?"

Conrad was going to answer when his father followed it up by asking him another question. "Did you get her pregnant?"

"Of course not," he answered defensively.

There were only two people in the world who truly intimidated Conrad—his father and, even more so, his mother. He had decided to tell his father first, hoping he would pass the news on to his mother, so she would have time to process it before he talked to her.

Conrad didn't get his wish, however, as his mother, a partner in the firm, had come into his father's office, reminding them that there were clients in the office waiting area.

"Please lower your voices. What is the problem, gentlemen?" his mother had asked, sounding more like she was speaking to colleagues than to family members. That was his mother.

Both men froze. Neither of them wanted to tell her. Finally, his father spoke.

"You got yourself into this, you tell her." The elder Kramer sat down and leaned back in his oversized, soft leather desk chair, turning the conversation over to Conrad, who quietly shared his news.

Now Conrad's mother was shouting, too. "Have you lost your mind? You have another year of law school, and then you'll join the firm—or are you going to give up on your dreams completely?"

Conrad rarely spoke up for himself when it came to his mother, but something came over him momentarily and he boldly asked, "Whose dreams are we talking about, Mother—mine, or yours?"

His mother looked at him with fierce, angry eyes, which always got to Conrad, and he settled back into his usual place. He lowered his voice. "I'm sorry, Mother. I'm not giving up on my dreams. I plan to finish law school, and Elizabeth will be starting law school soon herself," Conrad told his mother, hoping it would make things better.

"We're not finished discussing this," his mother said. "Dinner. Seven. Don't be late," she said coolly and walked out of the office, flashing a fake smile at the clients as she walked by them. She was a master of masking her true feelings, which was why she was such a cunning and successful attorney.

Conrad spent the late afternoon walking around the Lincoln Park Zoo, his go-to place to calm down and think since his teen years. Finally, he walked back to his car to warm up as he couldn't feel his fingers any longer. He had guessed correctly that his news would not be well-received. Perhaps, deep down, that was part of the appeal of getting engaged to someone he had only known for six weeks—of getting engaged to someone like Elizabeth.

Knowing there was no way to avoid it, he went home to face his parents. The family's housekeeper and cook, Laurette, hugged Conrad when he walked in from the back door of the beautiful three-story rowhouse. His body was cold and stiff from being outside for hours, but that didn't stop Laurette. She had been with the family for almost twenty years—since Conrad was in kindergarten. Laurette loved him, even though he wasn't always as nice to her as he should be. She seemed to understand that Conrad needed to take things out on someone, and patiently let his remarks slide, knowing they really weren't meant for her. She knew he was not a happy young man, even though he had every advantage in the world and was talented in so many areas of life. She also knew that those things didn't bring him—or anyone—true happiness.

Laurette had made his favorite meal this evening, yet he only ate a few bites of the savory chateaubriand and her special recipe of twice-baked potatoes. His parents had asked her to serve all the food items at once, then dismissed her. Laurette felt sorry for Conrad and gave him a pitiful glance as she made her way back to the kitchen.

Conrad's mother, Nina, was so angry she could barely speak, so Conrad's father began the talk—or, rather, the interrogation.

"How long have you known this girl?"

"Elizabeth is not a girl; she's a woman, a beautiful

woman I might add. I met her in a law school course that is also open to senior undergraduates. She will receive her Bachelor of Science in Social Work this May and is in the application process for law school." Conrad fudged that information a tad, but he knew the more likely it appeared that Elizabeth was truly going to law school in the fall, the more likely his parents might accept her.

"Social work!" his mother exclaimed. "I suppose she's one of those bleeding-heart public defender types." Her words dripped with utter disdain.

Always concerned about the Kramer image, his father asked, "And just where is this girl from, and what does her family do?"

"She is from a farming family in Iowa," Conrad replied softly.

His father was speechless.

His mother stared daggers at him, then finally spoke.

"I cannot look at you right now," she said matter-of-factly. She turned away from Conrad and took a sip from her glass of Dominus Cabernet Sauvignon.

"I will make that easier for you, Mother," Conrad said, taking the cloth napkin off his lap, patting his mouth with it, then dropping it onto his plate. He stood up and rushed out of the house to his car. He apologized to Laurette on his way through the kitchen, hot tears burning in his eyes.

Conrad knew he shouldn't drive a car in his current state of mind, but he had to get out of that toxic environment. He had known his parents would not approve of Elizabeth. She was everything they were not, and he was quite sure that was one of the reasons he had been attracted to her in the first place, and one of the things he loved best about her.

He wound the BMW through the neighborhood streets until he reached the ramp to the expressway, blasting Mötley Crüe, the music he listened to whenever he was upset. And Conrad was beyond upset. He hoped Elizabeth was having a better experience in Iowa. He had her parents' phone number, but he didn't want to call her on their home phone. He swore to himself the next thing he was going to buy his fiancée was a mobile phone. His did him little good if she didn't have one, too.

His *fiancée*. He let the word sink in.

In the back of his mind, his father's question haunted him. *What were you thinking?*

Elizabeth sat at the old oak farm table that had been in the family for generations. Her mother had prepared beef stew and biscuits for dinner and made brownies for dessert. As she sat, she fingered the ring in her jeans pocket. She would put it on after they ate. Elizabeth had thought about telling them right away when she got home that afternoon, but quickly thought better of it. She decided they might as well enjoy a meal before she dropped her unexpected news.

The meal was perfect, as usual. Her mother was a wonderful cook, and an equally wonderful person. Elizabeth had always been proud to be her daughter, as her mom usually spoke no ill of anyone. That changed in an instant this evening.

As they finished their last bites of brownie, her mother mentioned what a wonderful surprise it was to have

Elizabeth home, even if she could only stay until the next afternoon.

"Well, I have another surprise for you," Elizabeth said, digging into her pocket and pulling out the huge solitaire diamond ring, slipping it onto her left ring finger. "Surprise," she said.

"Is this some kind of joke?" her mother asked.

"No, it's real. I am engaged to Conrad. I know it's only been a couple of months, but we love each other. He asked me to marry him on Valentine's Day, and I said yes."

"Why would you do that, just when you're going to graduate and move back and be a social worker in Webster County?"

"That was one of my previous options, but my plans have changed. I hope to go to law school this fall," she stated.

"Law school! Just what the world needs, another greedy lawyer," her mother groaned.

Elizabeth was taken off guard by her mom's reaction and looked at her dad. She couldn't quite read his feelings until he spoke.

"I've got to get choring," he said. He did need to do chores, but not immediately. Doing farm work was her father's way of dealing with tough things that came his way, or when he didn't know what to say—or didn't want to say what he was thinking. He stood up and thanked his wife for supper and left the table, grabbing his chore coat from a hook near the back door as he exited the white-painted farmhouse.

Her mother became silent. That was the way she became whenever she was very angry. It was a rarity, but the family knew that if they received the "silent treatment," one was really in trouble with her. Her mom stood up and started clearing the table and Elizabeth helped cover the leftovers and put them in the fridge for lunch the next day.

They stood next to each other, her mom washing dishes and Elizabeth drying. Neither said a word the entire time. Elizabeth wiped the last pan, then dried the countertop near the sink.

Her mother headed to the living room, where she turned on the television and sat in her favorite chair, taking out her latest knitting project, which sat in a basket next to the crushed velvet chair.

Elizabeth sat down on the sofa, not knowing exactly what to do or say.

Her dad came in from the barn an hour later, washed up, and sat in his recliner in the living room, putting up the footrest. He took the latest copy of the *Farm Journal* from the table next to his chair and started reading.

Elizabeth had understood that her news might not be what her parents wanted to hear, but she wasn't prepared for such a cool response from these usually warm and embracing people. She had always felt loved—dearly. She also knew they were not used to any erratic behavior from her—that was her older brother's department. She was always the perfect one in their eyes, and she often tried to live up to this illusion, which was a difficult and dangerous way to live.

After an hour of silence except for the drone of the television, Elizabeth went upstairs to her room to go to bed and cried herself to sleep.

Chapter 12

Staring at the computer screen, Joe shook his head and emitted a heavy sigh. He'd spent the entire morning online with little to show for his efforts. He just didn't understand how there could be so little information about Pastor Kate on the internet. His next move was to search for the other names that came up with hers. He began to research Elizabeth Katherine Jones. There was a birth record for a person by that name in Fort Dodge, Iowa. The birth date seemed consistent with Pastor Kate's age. It showed other family members' names—Robert Jones, Sharon Jones, and Michael Jones. Since there was little on Elizabeth, he researched the others.

All were living, and all had the same address in Iowa. Robert and Sharon had no social media pages, but Michael had a Facebook page. Most of his posts were about sports, particularly his daughter's achievements in basketball and his son's in wrestling. There was one post with him and his wife and some family members at Christmas. He thought the older man had eyes that reminded him of Pastor Kate's, and the woman next to him looked like a more mature version of the pastor. It wasn't much to go on, but he had to begin somewhere.

Joe retrieved a phone number for the home and punched in the numbers. The phone rang and rang. There was no answering machine or voicemail. He was just about to stop the call when a woman finally answered.

"Jones residence," the woman said. The voice sounded like that of an older person. It also reminded him of the pastor's.

Joe explained who he was and asked if this was the former residence of Elizabeth Katherine Jones. The woman who had answered was quiet for a moment.

"I'm sorry, I can't help you," she finally said softly, with a shaky voice. Joe felt she was not being forthcoming, but he couldn't prove it. He quickly gave her his name again, department, and phone number, but the woman hung up mid-sentence.

He made some notes on the call and determined he would ask Pastor Kate about it when she was awake.

He was thinking about calling the hospital when the hospital called him. Pastor Kate had opened her eyes. They planned to wean her off the ventilator. Joe wished there wasn't so much snow outside, or he would go to the hospital immediately. He told the nurse he would stop in the next morning, but she interrupted him.

"Oh, by the way, a woman called late last night and said she was a family member. I told her that Kate was in the ICU but not awake yet. She said she would call back again. I was going to get her personal information so I could contact her, but she hung up."

Joe thought that was odd. Why would someone not leave their name or number? For a second, he thought about the woman at the Jones residence.

"Did the voice sound older or younger?"

"I'm not sure I can give an age, but on the younger side, I'd say."

"Let me know if the person calls again, and try to get a name and number," Joe said.

Joe sat thinking about it for a moment, wondering why the caller would not have left any contact information. It made him nervous. It just didn't seem right. Then he had another thought. What if the person calling had something to do with the shooting? He called the sheriff and told him he thought perhaps there should be an officer posted outside of Kate's room—just in case.

The sheriff thought it was a long shot and said that they were already short on personnel. He said he would check with the hospital and see if there was some way to monitor more closely anyone who came to see Kate in the future and see if they could have security stop by from time to time. It was not what Joe had wanted, but it was better than nothing. And he knew the sheriff was right—it might not be anything to worry about.

Joe looked outside. The snow had finally stopped falling, and he could hear a snowblower clearing out snow in his neighbor's driveway. He knew he would have to get out there soon with his shovel, too, and was not looking forward to it.

It took Joe almost an hour to shovel his short driveway. He decided he should investigate buying a snowblower one of these days. Then again, he often enjoyed the physical aspect of shoveling, except on days like this one, when the snow was wet, heavy, deep, and took twice as long as usual to clear.

Jodie met him in the kitchen as he entered from the attached garage. Her color was better than the day before, and she pulled him to herself for a kiss.

"Oh, your face is so cold!" Jodie exclaimed.

"Sorry about that," he said.

"Maybe I could warm you up," she said, a familiar glint in her eye.

Joe didn't hesitate a moment. It was a rare occasion that he and Jodie shared intimacy these days, and he wasn't going to pass up an opportunity.

Later, with Jodie's head on his chest, Joe caressed her arm with his strong, now warm hand.

"Maybe I should shovel snow more often," he remarked.

Jodie chuckled softly, then pulled his hand to her mouth and kissed it. "I love you, Joe."

"I love you, too, Jodie," he replied, and then added, "I'm glad you're feeling better today. I was worried about you yesterday."

"I think it was just the aftermath of all that happened at the dance. I kept thinking all day yesterday—what if one of those bullets had hit you?" she said, her voice breaking.

He turned to her, took her face in his hands, and kissed her softly and sweetly. He didn't say anything, but he had experienced the same thoughts throughout the day. What if he had been shot, or killed, leaving Jodie a widow and the baby without a father? He tried to put the idea out of his head.

"I just wish we had more to go on," Joe said, putting his head back down on the pillow. He told Jodie the little he had learned, ending with what the nurse had told him about the phone call from a supposed relative.

"That sounds suspicious to me, Joe. Why wouldn't the

woman identify herself and leave a number?"

"Exactly what I thought," he said and sighed. "And that woman in Iowa. She was holding out on me—I'm sure of it. I think I'll try to do more research on this Elizabeth Jones person."

"I'll help you. Let's get dressed," Jodie said, feeling eager and energized.

The two sat at the dining table, their laptops in front of them.

"This Elizabeth Jones is almost as difficult to research as Pastor Kate," Joe said after an hour. "It's like someone went into the files and had everything removed."

"Not everything," Jodie said with a smile on her face. She turned her laptop toward Joe so he could see a photo on it. "This is from a 4-H website in northwest Iowa, talking about its state champions over the years. This photo is from 1979. The members in this photo won blue ribbons at the State Fair. Anyone look familiar to you?"

Although the photo was of a twelve-year-old, the shape of her face, the rosy cheeks, and the bright blue eyes were ones he'd looked into often in the past few years. Joe's eyes widened as he looked at the photo.

"And it says the woman standing in the back row behind her is an adult leader, Sharon Jones. Isn't that the name of the woman you called in Iowa?"

"One and the same. The girl in the photo is named Elizabeth Jones, and she looks like she could be a young Pastor Kate. Sharon Jones is likely related to Elizabeth— possibly her mother, or an aunt. At the very least, she knew Elizabeth. Obviously, she didn't want to help me out. Or maybe she isn't in contact with Elizabeth anymore and didn't know what to say."

"Why would Pastor Kate change her name, or not be in contact with her family anymore?" Jodie wondered.

"Let's see what we can find." Joe looked back at his notes. "There was another name online—Elizabeth Katherine Kramer, and a Conrad Kramer, too. Both were listed as somehow connected to Elizabeth Jones. Let's see if there is anything online about them."

Again, it seemed there was little to be found about Elizabeth. Conrad, however, was another matter. There were numerous articles about him and some of the high-profile cases he had won in Chicago as a lawyer. Most of Conrad's successes involved getting business executives out of messy situations rather than criminal cases, although there were a few of those as well. One notable case made the news twice, once when Conrad got the man absolved of assault and battery in which a man nearly died. A year later, he defended the same man in another assault charge. That time, two people had been injured. The case ended up being settled out of court at the last minute.

Another article in *Chicago Magazine* highlighted the powerhouse Kramer family law firm. A photo came up of five people—three women and two men. Jodie gasped when she looked at the photo and read the caption below it saying that the firm had just expanded with its newest member, Conrad's wife, Elizabeth Katherine Kramer. And there she was—in her expensive business suit, her arms crossed over her chest like the other women in the photo, standing behind Conrad, who sat in a chair like his father. The woman was a younger version of Pastor Kate—but with long, thick blonde hair. Jodie wasn't certain if it was Kate at first, as her hair was now much shorter and graying and she was at least twenty pounds heavier, but the eyes gave it away again.

Jodie turned the laptop toward Joe.

"Anyone look familiar?"

Joe just stared for a moment, then turned to his laptop and typed in "Elizabeth Kramer, attorney at law." Nothing came up. Then he tried Conrad's name again, in a more personal format. He had a brief, failed marriage just two years after his and Elizabeth's divorce. Years later, he married a Genevieve Markwell, with whom he had a daughter, who was now a freshman in college. The records indicated they had recently divorced, as well.

"Someone did a good job expunging information about Elizabeth Kramer," Joe said. "It had to be someone with resources and know-how."

"Like some high-power lawyer or lawyers?" Jodie asked.

"Could very well be. But why? Did something happen that made the Kramer family disown her and want to disassociate from her? Or did *she* want nothing to do with the Kramer family after the divorce? Or perhaps she didn't want anyone in the church-world to know that she had been married once?"

"I suppose those could be possible reasons. Or maybe she didn't want people at church to know about her former career—even though I can't imagine that being an issue. I remember Pastor Kate talking about some of her seminary classmates' former lives. They came from many different backgrounds. She always said she thought it was a good thing to have people in the pulpit with varied life experiences. I never thought to ask her when she got into ministry, or what she had done before it. I just assumed she had always been a pastor."

"I guess we'll just have to wait for her to tell us herself," Joe said. "Hopefully, she will be in a position to answer some questions tomorrow. It still doesn't explain much about who would want to harm her, though."

"Hmmm. Maybe this does. It seems that Elizabeth Kramer once had a restraining order filed against her ex-husband, Conrad Kramer, shortly after the divorce was finalized. It was eventually dropped."

"I'll give him a call tomorrow after I talk to Pastor Kate and get more information. I should be able to reach him at his office on a Monday. But for now, let's heat up that frozen chili for supper and watch the game. I hope it's a decent contest this year." Joe loved football but despised lopsided or sloppily played games. He also desperately wanted something to take his mind off this case for a while, if that was even possible.

He never enjoyed it when unexpected things turned up about people he thought he knew, but this news was really throwing him off base. He hoped things would become clearer the next day. Maybe he was wrong about those photos being of Pastor Kate, but deep down, he knew it was her, and that she had once lived a completely different life.

Chapter 13

Joe felt relieved when he saw a security guard standing outside Pastor Kate's door. He felt less so when the guard told him she only checked in once an hour. She tried to vary the times of her stops, though, just in case someone was paying attention to them.

But it was an even bigger relief to Joe to see his pastor open her eyes and give him a little smile when he walked into the room. It was difficult to juxtapose the image of that self-confident, striking lawyer he had seen in the photo online, the strong leader who led their church community, with the frail, pale woman in the bed in front of him.

He stopped next to the bed and just looked at her for a moment.

"I must look really bad," she said.

"No, it's not that. You look like anyone who just got shot and had surgery would look..." His voice trailed off.

She turned her head away from Joe's gaze and spoke even more quietly. "You know, don't you?"

"Well, I know you haven't always been Kate Roberts, and you haven't always been a pastor, if that's what you are asking. I was kind of hoping you would fill me in—especially if there's someone you can think of who would like to hurt you."

"Unfortunately, I can think of quite a few people who might want to hurt me, although I never really thought it could come to this."

"I'm listening," Joe said, pulling a chair to the bedside.

"You're going to need something to write all of this down, and the time to do it."

Joe took out his tablet and got ready to take notes.

"Ready when you are."

Over the next two hours, Joe made notes as Pastor Kate shared about her past. She began with the story about meeting Conrad her senior year of college, the engagement, and how it changed everything in her life, especially her career path and her family relations. Her parents could not seem to accept her decision to marry someone like Conrad, especially her mother. Her father just quietly went along with all of it.

She had once been close to her brother, Mike, when they were young, but each had different interests in high school and their paths diverged.

Mike stayed home to work on the family farm while Elizabeth went off to college. They were never as close again. But when Elizabeth married Conrad and moved to Chicago, the entire family simply fell apart. Her mother's last words to her were to call if she ever came to her senses.

She had married Conrad in a private ceremony in Chicago, followed by a gathering at his parents' club for two hundred of their closest associates, friends, and a few members of the extended Kramer family. There were white linen tablecloths, white roses on each table, and a string quartet played throughout the cocktail hour and dinner. Neither of them wanted that type of wedding or celebration, but people didn't say no to the Kramers, especially not to Conrad's mother.

She told the young couple it was the least they could do, considering this entire marriage was a thoughtless act. Conrad's father had convinced his wife they should support the marriage on some level and host a nice wedding reception, if not for any other reason but to save face with their acquaintances. He told his wife that if they didn't show some type of support, Conrad might do something even more embarrassing like eloping or, worse yet, leaving the area and the firm.

The evening went off splendidly. The Kramers knew how to pretend—they were masters of it. They told everyone how excited they were about Conrad marrying Elizabeth and announced proudly that she would be joining the family firm as soon as she graduated at the top of her class the next year—something that was actually true.

Elizabeth joined the firm upon graduation, even though she didn't care for the types of cases they tended to take on. She had to admit that the lifestyle it afforded was quite enjoyable, however, and that helped make her personal discomfort begin to fade away. Their wedding gift from his parents was the down payment on a house. The Kramers couldn't have their son living just anywhere. There was a honeymoon to St. Lucia, "his and hers" Mercedes, and, of course, a top-tier wardrobe. One must look like a winner to be a winner in court, according to Kramer Law.

Things weren't too bad for the first six months of marriage, although Conrad still dictated too much of Elizabeth's life. Still, Elizabeth was in love, and told herself he would eventually change. But he didn't. He only seemed to get more and more controlling as time went on. Conrad would call and text her non-stop when he wasn't in court. He often popped in unannounced in her office, just when she was finally getting some work done. At first it seemed cute, but not after a year of it. She talked to him about it, but it seemed like he only got worse after that. He accused her of having something to hide, which wasn't true.

But that wasn't the main reason their marriage eroded and eventually ended. Conrad had made Elizabeth second chair in a case defending the son of a wealthy acquaintance, a man named John Germaine, who was facing an aggravated assault charge. She didn't want to work on the case, especially since she didn't feel the man was innocent, and he made her feel very uncomfortable. But Conrad just wouldn't stop hounding her about it, so she gave in and worked the case with him. And she did her very best—unfortunately. There was an issue with the prosecution's evidence that she discovered, and that helped seal Conrad's win on the case.

Conrad was elated over the win, but Elizabeth felt bad about it. She just hoped her gut instinct about their client was wrong. She never felt the same about work after that case. She hated going into the office. She hated everything Kramer Law stood for. She told Conrad about her feelings, hoping he would have some sympathy, but just the opposite occurred. For the first time, he was truly mean to her. He was never physically abusive, but his verbal and emotional abuse sprang into action. According to Conrad, everything she did was wrong. His controlling and accusatory behavior became stronger than ever, too.

Elizabeth had wanted to go to counseling, but he said that was for weak people. She didn't know what to do and decided that if her personal life wasn't going to change, her professional one would. She applied for and was immediately hired as an Assistant District Attorney for the county, taking about a half-million dollar a year pay cut in the process.

Conrad was furious at her decision to leave the firm, and very hurt, too. His parents were out-of-this-world livid. The things they said took years of therapy to process. District Attorneys were the enemies of Kramer Law, and Elizabeth wasn't even a full-fledged one, only an assistant. They accused her of taking the position just to embarrass the Kramer family.

So, things got worse and worse every day at home. One morning, she went to the garage to drive to work and found her car gone. She thought it had been stolen, or perhaps Conrad had taken it in to be serviced, until Conrad informed her she'd have to buy a different one. The other one had been sold. Elizabeth never replaced it, but instead started walking to the "L" station and riding the train to work each day.

While it wasn't glamorous, she could live with the work she now did every day, and thus live with herself as a human being. She also felt more physically fit than she had in years. Another perk was that it kept her out of the house for longer periods of time, away from the hostile voice of her husband and her interfering in-laws. She and her husband ate separately, and Conrad slept hugging his side of the bed every night. Elizabeth did the same.

The real end came six months later. It turned out her instincts were spot-on about John Germaine, the man she had helped clear of aggravated assault. This time he injured two people. One was a supposed friend of his whom he had beaten in a fight, the other an innocent bystander who was simply in the wrong place at the wrong time. The cases came up in the docket at the D.A.'s office and Elizabeth was assigned to represent the two victims. She thought about recusing herself, but then thought that it was a way for her to make amends for helping free the perpetrator the first time.

The Kramers went ballistic. It was the ultimate affront to their firm and to their family. Conrad represented the defendant once again and pulled out all the stops. He, along with his sister, buried Elizabeth in court, and her clients ended up taking a plea deal, which was ridiculous. She felt terrible that she hadn't received real justice for her clients. The bystander was a simple laborer who couldn't work temporarily because of his injuries. He had to go on disability. He had been forcefully knocked into while the other men fought, injuring his back and shoulder. His disability payments barely covered living expenses for himself, his wife, and his twin daughter and son. Kate remembered his name was Brian Banyon. He and the other victim were awarded ten thousand dollars each for their pain and inconvenience, but that wouldn't last very long for a family of four living in the city.

Kate told Joe that either of them might still be quite unhappy with her. And about the look John Germaine gave her when she went up against him in court, instead of defending him the second time, Kate said, "He looked like he could have killed me."

The week after the case was settled, Elizabeth filed for a divorce and then gave notice at the D.A.'s office. She had one more case she had to finish some work on, and then she was done. As she packed the contents of her small desk into a box, she wished she had gotten her master's in social work instead of a law degree. She also wished she had never met Conrad Kramer.

Joe took down the names of the Kramer family members and any personal contact information she might have for them. He would begin with Conrad Kramer, whom he already did not like, even though he had never met him.

While he didn't want to completely exhaust the pastor, whose eyes were now getting heavy, he quickly asked about the others who might be upset enough with her to want to hurt her. Kate told him about another case she had worked on at Kramer Law, which didn't end well, and the losing party had threatened her. It was a long time ago, but she would never forget it. The man had lost his business because of her defense of her client. However, the last she knew, he had started a new business, and it had skyrocketed, so perhaps he had gotten over his feelings of hatred for her.

She also said there could be people at any of the churches she had served. She had become an interim pastor who specialized in serving congregations where there had been a pastor removed for some sort of impropriety, usually of a sexual nature. She mentioned that when she arrived, she would deal with a variety of emotions among the church members. Some people were very sad, while others felt betrayed. And then there were those members who had become friends with male pastors who had been let go for inappropriate relationships with female members of the church. They often felt enraged and indignant, feeling their pastor friend was not being treated fairly and didn't need to be reprimanded or removed.

In almost every congregation she had served, there

had been someone who stormed out of her office or left the congregation, often taking a number of other members with them. They had been so enamored with their former pastor that they could forgive anything the person had done, and just wanted things to go back to the way they used to be, even in the face of actual evidence of wrongful behavior. They would have done anything to keep their beloved pastor, no matter what he had done. Pastor Kate provided the name of one of the people who had been the most vocal and hostile.

When Pastor Kate said those were the ones who first came to mind, Joe was amazed at the list he had before him. He would share this information with his colleagues as soon as he left the hospital, so they could begin to investigate.

Joe finished his notes and stood, putting his tablet under his arm and stretching his legs, his joints rejoicing at moving again. He wasn't quite certain what to say to Pastor Kate, and she sensed it, as she always seemed to do.

"I know it's a lot to process, Joe. Just keep in mind that people who become pastors are human beings, too, and we were young and naive once upon a time. We made, and still make, mistakes—even some whoppers," Kate said, with the voice of someone stripped of her dignity.

"I hear you, Pastor Kate," Joe responded. He nodded his head to her and started for the door, then stopped and turned back to her. "Same for people who become cops, too. See you later," he said.

"See you later, Joe. Thanks for coming," she said, tears stinging her eyes.

Joe had to get out of there. And he had to get to the bottom of this. No one deserves to be shot, even someone who may have made mistakes in the past. And especially someone who had helped so many individuals and congregations get back on their feet for so many years. And most certainly no one who had helped his beloved wife—or himself—as much as Pastor Kate.

Chapter 14

The sun was shining brightly when Joe left the hospital, making the top layer of snow glisten like diamonds under a jeweler's light. Joe wished it could have been like this the day before, so people could have enjoyed the snow on a day many were off from work. Instead, the entire weekend had been a trial for everyone in southern Wisconsin, and especially the residents of Farmerton.

Between the shooting and the snowstorm, the community felt shocked, like they had taken another communal gut punch. There had been a somber air about town when Joe had driven down the main street earlier that morning, heading for Madison. It was a complete reversal of the atmosphere only days earlier on Valentine's Day.

He looked at the dark windows of Sissy's Scissors, which would be open the next day, but only operated by the two other hairstylists. Sissy had come home from the hospital late the prior afternoon but was on strict orders to take it easy for at least one week. She had a follow-up appointment scheduled then, and the doctor would reevaluate her situation at that time.

Sissy had called Joe first thing that morning to inform him that she sure hoped she would be able to go back to work the next week, or there may be another incident in town. Her husband was driving her crazy with all his hovering and constant concern. She knew he was only trying to be kind and loving, but that wasn't helping her in the moment. Even her confession to him about her gambling and money problems hadn't stopped him. One good thing Jon had done, however, was to call a friend who was an accountant. The man was scheduled to visit them at their home the next day to make a workable plan to get Sissy out of her predicament.

Joe called Conrad Kramer's office several times after leaving Pastor Kate, but the administrative assistant kept saying the same thing. He was either in a meeting, or he was unavailable to talk. Yes, he was in the office, and would be all day, but his schedule was packed.

Joe thought about his options, and decided he was going to Chicago, which he didn't relish. It would take up most of the rest of his day, but he *was* going to see Conrad Kramer, one way or the other. He'd question him, then he'd get back to Jodie, who seemed to have more energy this morning than she had over the weekend. It seemed like some of the trauma was subsiding, and she felt more like herself. He had been concerned about her, especially on Saturday when she was so tired. Then again, he had read women often experienced a lot of fatigue late in pregnancy. He'd just never been through any of this before, so he was often quick to worry and even hover at times. He smiled as he thought about Sissy's husband doing the same thing to her. Joe could "feel his pain."

Joe detested driving on the expressway into Chicago. Either one was flying at a ridiculous speed with vehicles weaving between lanes, coming within inches of one another, or one moved like a snail in bumper-to-bumper traffic.

Today's journey had been a bit of both. Once he took the Ohio Street exit, traffic improved. He was reminded why many people who worked downtown used mass transit.

Joe was amazed at the impressive row of law firms on LaSalle Street. It was certainly a different world than the one he lived in. Farmerton had no traffic lights and no building above two stories. The highest structures were the water tower and the peak of the feed mill.

After finding a parking ramp down the street, he walked to the firm. He checked his service weapon at the main desk of the building and took an elevator to the top floor of the glass and steel twelve-story building. He showed his credentials at the receptionist's desk at Kramer Law. The woman told him she would tell Mr. Kramer that he was here to see him, but wasn't sure when, or if, he could fit him in. Joe decided he would wait at the desk until she picked up the phone and called the man, just to make certain she announced his arrival.

"Mr. Kramer will see you in ten to fifteen minutes, Sergeant," she said coolly. "You can have a seat, if you'd like."

Joe really wasn't eager to sit again after the long car ride, but he reluctantly sat down in a plush chair, surveying the reception area. Paintings of city scenes adorned the walls. Objects of art stood in corners or on the end tables, all of which looked expensive. It was clear to Joe he was in a high-end establishment.

After ten minutes, the receptionist came to him and told him to follow her. They walked down the hall to the first office on the left. The woman opened the door, stepped in, and announced him, then stepped back and turned to Joe, informing him he could now enter.

Joe suppressed a whistle as he entered the impressive office. Floor-to-ceiling windows on two sides made for quite the view of downtown and Lake Michigan. The other walls were covered with photos, some with politicians and celebrities, others with the family members in the firm.

"Officer," Conrad said, stepping out from behind his huge mahogany desk and holding out a hand to shake.

Joe took the man's hand, looking into his eyes. They were the bluest eyes he had ever seen, and Joe supposed he must be wearing tinted contacts. But despite their bright color, they also looked tired. Joe did know that being a lawyer involved many hours of work, so that made sense.

Conrad instructed him to have a seat in one of two gray leather chairs and returned to his oversized, black leather manager's chair behind the desk.

"What can I do for you, Sergeant?"

"I'm investigating a case involving someone you might be familiar with—a Kate Roberts?"

Joe was expecting Conrad to say he didn't know Kate, as she had changed her name and he wasn't sure Conrad was aware of that, or if he did know, to try to pretend he didn't. Joe was quite adept at knowing when someone was being genuine or not and searched the man's face.

Conrad's eyes flew open and seemed filled with fear. "Is she okay? Did something happen to her?"

"So, you do know her?"

"Kate used to be my wife—although her name was Elizabeth at that time. Again, did something happen to her?"

Joe waited a moment, wanting to see what Conrad might say of his own volition. Conrad was silent.

"Is there some reason you would suspect something

might happen to her?" Joe asked.

"Not particularly, but please, is she okay?" Conrad asked, his eyes starting to mist.

"It is believed she will make a full recovery, but she was recently the victim of a violent crime," Joe said.

"What sort of violent crime?"

Joe decided to tell him, as he appeared more agitated by the second. He didn't want someone suffering a coronary during an interview.

"She sustained a gunshot wound."

"Oh, my god! Where and when did this occur?" he asked as he stood up, then began to pace back and forth behind his desk. "Elizabeth—no, no! Who would do such a thing?" Conrad asked, his face red and a vein throbbing in his temple.

"That's what I'm here to ask you, frankly."

Conrad sat back down, stroking his thick, mostly blond hair back, over and over. This man was a wreck, but Joe needed to ask him more.

"Let's discuss the possibilities," Joe said calmly.

Conrad took two deep, slow breaths, then blew them out of his mouth, a common tool used for calming oneself. "Okay," he finally said.

"You said you wonder who could have done such a thing, Mr. Kramer. Would you take a moment and think of someone who might wish her harm—someone who greatly disliked her, or a client who was dissatisfied with her work?"

Conrad took a drink of water from a large glass water bottle, then closed his eyes.

"My family never accepted Elizabeth, but that was all a long time ago. I don't think any of them know of her name change, or at least we have never discussed it. I can give you my parents' contact information, if you wish. My sister is out of the office right now, but I'll give you her personal phone number and let her know to expect a call, so she picks up. Clients—I can't really think of any off the top of my head. Elizabeth was a brilliant lawyer," he said.

He sounded so sincere that Joe had to remind himself that this was a man who had dished out years of emotional abuse, and who had once had a restraining order filed against him. He also knew he was a great lawyer and could most likely put on quite a convincing act if he cared to.

"You say you were aware of Elizabeth's name change. Were you also aware of where she was living or where she was working?"

"Yes, and yes. I found out last Valentine's Day," Conrad said quietly.

Joe's eyes grew wide when he heard Conrad's answer but remained calm. "Valentine's Day—that's very specific. Is there a reason for knowing that exact date?"

Conrad looked sad. "Yes. I remember the day because I thought it seemed very appropriate that I got a report on her whereabouts on that day, as I always think of Elizabeth every Valentine's Day. We were engaged on Valentine's Day—a long time ago."

"And how did you feel when you finally found her? Did you make any attempts to contact her?"

"I haven't contacted her, although it made me feel better to know that she was alive, and not far away. I just wanted to know that she was okay. She was the love..." Conrad stopped himself.

"And you did not share the information with anyone else?"

"No one."

Joe flipped a page in his notebook. He liked to do things old school, especially in important cases when details really mattered. Later, he would make a board to help him see the entire picture more clearly.

"Do the names Theodore Gavin or Brian Banyon stand out to you?" Joe inquired.

"I can't say they do," Conrad responded.

"How about John Germaine?" Joe asked.

A look of recognition crossed Conrad's face this time. "Yes, I remember John. Elizabeth and I both worked on his assault case."

"She told me that. She also said that it was the case that changed her career—and her life—as she couldn't live with herself after getting him off, especially when he later injured two other men, Theodore Gavin and Brian Banyon. She also mentioned that your firm made certain she didn't get justice for them."

Conrad's complexion became scarlet. "Oh," he said softly. "Those were their names. I had forgotten." He sat quietly for a moment. "That was a very long time ago. It was during a very low period of my life. I was not a healthy person back then, or else..." Conrad didn't finish his thought. "Do you think they might be capable of doing her harm?"

"I suppose it's possible, but I don't know how they would know how to find her. It took all my resources to find out what had happened to her, and I have a lot of resources. I can't give you any contact information on them, but I'm sure you could find that."

"Anyone else you can think of?"

"Not at the moment, but I could call you if I think of anyone else," Conrad said.

Joe handed him his card. "By the way, Mr. Kramer, could you tell me your whereabouts this past Friday evening?"

Conrad pulled out his phone and looked at it. "This past Friday evening—I was with my sister and her family—her husband and son now work for the firm—at the museum's fundraiser for Val..." He stopped and gathered his wits about him. "The shooting happened on Valentine's Day?" he asked, seeming emotional again.

"Yes. And I assume there are other witnesses to your attendance, other than your family members?"

"Yes, and there is video evidence, as well, as there are security cameras all over the museum."

"I will check on it, to be sure. And I will be in contact with your sister via the phone, but I would assume she would have many witnesses and be on the security feed as well."

"Yes, that is correct."

"Did your parents attend the fundraiser?"

"No, my mother had a cold and didn't feel up to it. My father stayed home with her."

Joe knew where his next stop would be.

"Thank you for the information, Mr. Kramer. I will be in touch."

"Is Elizabeth—Kate—still hospitalized?"

"I can't share that information."

"I understand," Conrad said. "I will call you if I think of anyone else. I'm also going to do some checking on those people you mentioned."

"As will I."

Conrad shook Joe's hand again, and then the sergeant was gone. Conrad sat down in his soft, oversized leather chair and put his head in his hands on the desktop. "Please don't let anything happen to Elizabeth," he said to no one.

In his mind, he was transported back to their first Valentine's Day, when he proposed. That winter, he had been saving some of his allowance every month to go on a spring ski trip out west, and for a trip to Europe with friends in between the semester and his summer internship. But instead, he had fallen head-over-heels in love, and all those plans were quickly dropped.

All he had been able to think of, day and night, was Elizabeth. It was a wonder he was still doing well in school, but quite frankly, he hadn't found law school as challenging as he thought it would be. His classmates were always grumbling about how long it took them to read their assignments or finish a paper. Conrad would shake his head in agreement, even though it only took him half the time it did for most. He guessed he had inherited *something* good from his parents—a quick and brilliant legal brain. Other than that, the things they passed on were not in his favor, especially when it came to relationships.

Conrad thought about Elizabeth—or Kate, as she preferred to be named now—in a hospital bed somewhere, and his eyes clouded. Then he slowly opened a lower drawer in his desk and reached toward the back. He gently pulled out a soft, red knit scarf and held it to his face, taking in her scent. "Elizabeth," he said softly.

Chapter 15

Joe was not prepared for the neighborhood surrounding the Kramer family home. Their street was composed of unique three-story stone rowhouses. Joe could almost smell the money. He had called ahead to make certain someone would be home, and they had given him permission to park in a spot in the alley behind their home reserved only for residents and their guests.

After parking, Joe pressed a button near the iron gate leading onto the property. A young, accented voice answered and buzzed him in. He walked past a garage to his left, then through a yard that barely had any snow on it, and soon found himself on a completely cleared patio area with a built-in grill and fireplace. The outdoor furniture was currently covered but was still accessible. Joe noticed two balconies above, protruding from the upper floors.

He stood at the door until a petite Latina woman timidly opened it and quietly ushered him in. Her eyes widened in what Joe perceived as fear when she saw his uniform. She led him through the room, which was a combination laundry and mudroom.

The young woman led him down a hallway past a huge kitchen, where something delectable was cooking on the built-in stove in the center of a quartz island. Joe's next stop would be at a drive-through restaurant somewhere, and he hoped his stomach would not growl during his interview. They passed by a formal dining room until they reached their destination.

The Kramers were waiting for him in the streetside of the house, in a huge living room spanning the width of the home. It looked newly decorated in various shades of white and gray. Mr. and Mrs. Kramer sat at opposite ends of a sectional couch.

They didn't even stand up when Joe entered; rather, Mr. Kramer told Joe to have a seat in a chair, and then dismissed the young woman, whose name Joe learned was Cara.

"What might we do for you, Sergeant?" Mrs. Kramer asked. She was a striking woman. Her once-blonde hair had now turned silver, but it was thick and perfectly coiffed. She didn't seem old enough to have a son Conrad's age.

"I'm wondering if you may know a Kate Roberts?"

They both had blank expressions on their faces. There was no flicker of recognition as there had been with their son.

"Should we?" Nina asked after thinking about it for a moment.

"How about Elizabeth Katherine Jones?"

Now Joe saw recognition on both of their faces. The evidently faked smile on Mrs. Kramer's lips turned into an angry scowl.

"We know her. What would you like to know about that"—she hesitated for a moment, trying to gather her wits about her and choose her words wisely—"that woman?"

"Have you been in contact with her lately?" Joe asked.

"Why on earth would anyone in our family want to

have contact with *her*? We have no idea where she is, and we have no desire to—*ever*," Nina continued.

"You seem to feel very strongly about her," Joe said.

"That would be putting it mildly. Elizabeth was the biggest mistake our son ever made. He was never the same person after meeting her—never the brilliant lawyer he could have been," she said. She was seething.

"Do you see things the same way, Mr. Kramer?" Joe asked, turning to him. It was as if Joe was looking at Conrad twenty-five years into the future.

Christian Kramer looked like he was preparing to speak but was cut off by his wife.

"Why are you asking us about Elizabeth?" Nina asked.

"She was the victim of a violent crime."

"And how would this be relevant to us?"

"You had both planned to attend a fundraiser last Friday evening, but you stayed home instead. Is that correct?"

"Yes. I was ill," Nina responded.

"Is there anyone who could corroborate this?"

"Cara was here until six o'clock," Nina said. "We also have a security system, which would show if we left the premises. You are welcome to view the footage, but do it before the end of the week, or it will be erased. If you leave your card, I will forward you the security company's information."

"Thank you, I'll do that."

"You can't possibly believe we had anything to do with that woman being harmed? We don't even know where she lives, and don't care to know," Nina continued.

"I'm just doing my job, ma'am. Surely you can appreciate that," Joe said. He turned to Mr. Kramer again.

"And this information is correct, Mr. Kramer?"

This time Christian just nodded in agreement with Nina. It was clear that he wasn't in the habit of disagreeing with his wife, and he was definitely not the family spokesperson.

"Is there anyone you can think of who may have wanted to harm Elizabeth?"

"I would imagine there could be many disgruntled former clients, especially once she left our firm. But I do not know of anyone when she was working for us," Nina answered.

"If you do think of someone, please let me know," Joe said, handing her his business card.

"Of course," Nina responded, reaching for a small brass bell that sat on an end table near her. In a flash, Cara entered the room. Joe had thought that people rang bells for servants only in the movies, but here it was in real life.

"Cara, please see the officer out."

Cara's gaze was lowered. "Yes, ma'am."

Joe followed Cara down the hall. Once they reached the mudroom and were out of earshot of the Kramers, Joe turned to Cara to ask about Friday night. When he asked if he could ask her a question, she looked like she was ready to bolt out the door. When he inquired about the Kramers and Valentine's Day, she looked very relieved and said that it was correct that Mr. and Mrs. Kramer were home, and that Mrs. Kramer hadn't felt well. She seemed truthful, although Joe couldn't imagine Cara disagreeing with Mrs. Kramer on any issue. He figured that few people disagreed with Nina Kramer, and he imagined she had been a daunting adversary in the courtroom at one point in time.

Joe walked to his vehicle, amazed at how mild the temperature was outside compared to back home. He opened the door, slid into the seat, and googled fast food options nearby, as he was ravenous. He would call Conrad's sister, Katrina, on his way to his food stop. He hoped Conrad had contacted her and that he didn't have to spend the entire trip home playing phone tag.

After deciding on a sub sandwich shop with a drive-through, he called Katrina. It went to voicemail. He wondered if Conrad was speaking with her, or perhaps the elder Kramers were busy giving her a "heads up." Then he called the sheriff's office, asking his favorite technology deputy to obtain the surveillance videos at the museum and the Kramers' home and to send them to him.

That made Joe think about his uncomfortable visit with Nina and Christian, and he thought about what it must be like to have parents like the Kramers. They reminded him of his paternal grandfather, who had been a verbally and emotionally abusive man. His grandmother had done her best to shield her son, Joe's dad, from some of his wrath by sending him to live at her parents' farm during the summers. Joe's dad had also worked as many hours as he could get away with during the school year, staying out of his father's path—and thus his destructive behavior—as much as possible.

Joe imagined that Conrad and his sister had few opportunities to get away, although maybe they were lucky enough to go to a summer camp when they were children. He hoped so—for their sakes.

Joe finally connected with Katrina Kramer. She reiterated that she had been with Conrad, her husband, and her son at the fundraiser at the museum on Valentine's Day evening. She mentioned that there would be video evidence to support this, and Joe told her he would be checking with the security office as soon as possible.

When asked if she could think of anyone who would want to harm Elizabeth, Katrina said she did not, but then added, "but she was a bitch, so it's not that surprising to me."

Again, Joe just couldn't fathom anyone calling the woman he knew as Pastor Kate that word. She had always been just the opposite to everyone in Farmerton. He thought about how the pastor had counseled his wife—and himself, on occasion. He thought about her making funeral arrangements for the young man who had abducted Jodie when no one else in the world cared about him. He thought about the pastor's forgiving words as they scattered his ashes, ones of hope and of new creation.

Joe finally got his turkey sub and a cup of coffee, then followed his GPS to the freeway. At least this time he was heading out of the city, happy it was well before the afternoon rush hour. He decided he would stop again to see Pastor Kate, just briefly. He felt bad about the less-than-warm way he had treated her earlier, and hoped she would forgive him. Although knowing her, she probably already had.

Joe also felt he needed some positive vibes after being around the negativity of the Kramer household. He felt very grateful at that moment for his own very simple life.

Chapter 16

Pastor Kate smiled when Joe walked through the door. He had called and told the nurse to tell her he would be stopping back once again. He instantly felt relief at the sight of color coming back into her cheeks, her smile, and a little bit of the usual sparkle in her eyes. They, too, were very blue, which made him think about Conrad.

He had decided he would stay very briefly and avoid talking about Conrad, but he was the first thing she asked about.

"So, were you able to talk to Conrad?"

"Yes. I will let you know when his alibi is confirmed, but I don't think he was involved in harming you."

"Check carefully. He, and his entire family, can be very deceptive and persuasive."

"I promise I will. Now, how about you? How are you feeling?"

"More awake, but I also started to hurt more as the day has progressed. When I used to visit church members in the hospital after surgeries, they would always tell me the third day was the worst. I think some of the pain meds from the surgery start to wear off, and the reality of what has happened to one's body sets in, too.

She looked wistful. "I thought I was getting out of shape because it's harder to walk in winter, but now, it's going to be even worse. I'm not used to being 'down.' I'm used to being the strong one—physically and mentally.

Frankly, I'm worried I won't be able to get it all back, Joe. I'm not sure how I'll ever feel like me again."

"Don't count yourself out yet, Pastor Kate. It's only been a few days. I know it's not the same, but think about how far Jodie has come in the last year and a half. Just make sure you find someone good to talk to about all of this, even when the physical wounds are healed."

"You would make a good counselor, Joe."

"I had a good example. Just hang in there, okay?"

"Okay." She sighed.

"I should be going. I'm sure the beltline will be a beast."

"Drive carefully, Joe, and give that lovely wife of yours a hug for me."

"Will do, and will do," he said, and squeezed her hand as he stood to leave.

Again, Joe was mystified as he left. Who on earth would want to hurt—even kill—this person?

Joe called Jodie as he left the hospital, letting her know he was on his way home. He asked if there was anything he could bring home, but Jodie said she had made a pot of chicken noodle soup. For some reason, not only had it sounded good to her, but she had enough energy to make it.

Joe told her about his day, mentioning that he didn't think the Kramers had been involved in the shooting.

"Maybe not," Jodie said, "but they don't sound like the type of people who would dirty their own hands. They sound like the types who can pay for whatever they want, including hiring a shooter."

Of course, Jodie was right. "Good call. I'll check financial records tomorrow and see if there are any unusually large payments to anyone."

"You owe me."

"Understood. One neck and shoulder rub coming up." It used to be back rubs, or even a full-body massage, but not these days when Jodie was so uncomfortable. She mentioned more often in the past few weeks how she couldn't wait to have her body back to normal. For purely selfish reasons, Joe couldn't wait, either.

The next morning at the department, Joe watched the surveillance video from the museum fundraiser. It was clear that Conrad, Katrina, her husband—Robert Kramer-Holt—and son—Richard Kramer-Holt—were all in attendance. There was no way any of them could have been the shooter. He also saw evidence that no one left the elder Kramer's home, although he didn't believe either of them could have physically done it, even though they were in good shape for their ages.

Joe had an officer working on financial data, so he decided to call Terrence Tyson, the church council president in southeastern Iowa, who had detested Pastor Kate. The man agreed to meet with Joe later that afternoon. Joe decided to stop in at Bud's Diner for a quick, early lunch before hitting the road for the interview.

There was a certain comfort in stopping in at Bud's. Not only was there amazing home cooking to be had, but the people there were like family. Some even had their "own" table, just like people had their "own" pew at church, which they regularly claimed.

Joe took a spot at the counter, freeing up a table for others. He glanced up as the table behind him filled with the workers from the feed mill—minus Clifford, the farmer, this time.

"So, wasn't that the craziest Valentine's Day Ball? I didn't think I'd live to see the day when something like that happened in Farmerton. And what a mess it's made for the high school and the Fire and Rescue. They are trying to get everything out of the gym as quickly as possible so the basketball team can practice. I heard there's a good chance they can set up in a vacant warehouse and have the auction sometime this weekend for the items that weren't already sold—which was most of them. The band even offered to come back for free to play. The fire chief and a few other volunteers offered to be the auctioneers, and the church women of the area said they would make punch and pies. Too many people don't use the internet, so they nixed the online auction idea. They want to give everyone a chance to bid on items," a man in red flannel said.

"That's great, although I can't believe they will do as well as they had hoped," another mentioned.

"Speaking of doing well. I wonder how ol' Cliffy is doing, his sweetie being shot and all," the third man said.

Joe's head jerked around when he heard these words, and he almost dumped his spoon full of soup on his uniform shirt. Clifford's "sweetie" was Pastor Kate! He couldn't fathom it, but he would check it out as soon as he could.

The third man continued, "At least he wasn't there to see her lying on the floor and hauled out of there on a stretcher."

"Let's change the subject," the first man said. "I don't want to lose my appetite talking about someone getting shot."

That was a good idea, but it was already too late for Joe. He ate his soup as quickly as possible, of course, burning his tongue in the process. Now it would sting all afternoon, especially when he would have his afternoon cup of coffee.

Joe asked for his check, laid a bill on the counter, and told the waitress to keep the change. He needed to speak to Pastor Kate, but he had other business to attend to.

The day was warming up, and snow began melting along the edges of the sidewalk, revealing the tiniest bit of grass. This time of year was one of unpredictable weather, with possible swings in temperature of twenty or more degrees. Today Joe just wished it would make up its mind and stay decent until after the baby was born next month. He hoped they wouldn't have some crazy snowstorm when the time came—March could be even worse than February for unusual weather patterns. He didn't want to have to white-knuckle it to the hospital with a wife in labor.

The reality of the closeness of March weighed on Joe. It made him feel excited. It also made him nervous. And darn— he still hadn't gotten that crib put together. The entire weekend's plans had been completely interrupted. He would have to get to it soon, even though it would be tough with this unsolved shooting case going on.

Joe started the cruiser and headed out of Farmerton, tuning southwest on a county road toward the Iowa border. He wasn't looking forward to another road trip after his excursion the day before, although this one would be different than going into downtown Chicago. This man lived in the country. There wouldn't be a traffic issue, but it might pose its own challenges.

After a scenic hour-long drive, Joe turned into a driveway, which almost looked like a road. There were two large brick pillars on the sides of the entrance, which supported an ornate wrought-iron arch with the name "Tyson" in the center.

The driveway was paved and had been completely cleared of snow. Joe proceeded slowly, taking in the beauty of the woods around him on both sides. He finally approached a huge yard area. There was an outbuilding to one side, which looked big enough to house a good number of vehicles, including recreational ones. An area with a rock wall was in the center of a circle drive. An American flag flew from a tall flagpole.

Joe followed the drive around to the house. The yard—and house—were larger than any he had ever seen in a rural area. He guessed the home to be close to eight thousand square feet. Constructed of a light-colored brick, an arched porch and arched doorway greeted Joe. He rang the doorbell. He half expected a servant to open the door, but instead, Terrence Tyson answered, looking like he was in a magazine ad for Brooks Brothers clothing.

"Come in, come in, Officer. Welcome to my humble abode," Tyson remarked.

Joe almost rolled his eyes. He looked around the foyer, which was larger than his living room. It was a unique mix of rustic and chic, with a huge spiral staircase leading upstairs.

Terrence Tyson led Joe into a room at the back of the home that had huge windows overlooking a breathtaking view of the woods. Joe thought the view behind his house was nice, but this seemed almost otherworldly, especially after the weekend snowfall. Tall pine branches were covered in snow. They almost seemed fake, except for the snow, which was beginning to melt and drop to the ground in huge white clumps.

There were taxidermy mounts high on the walls of the room. Mr. Tyson had certainly landed some impressive bucks. Several antique rifles were displayed as well. Joe was certain this man would be the owner of a thirty-caliber rifle.

"Could I get you something to drink, Officer—a cocktail, or maybe a beer? The little woman is playing bridge, so I won't get into trouble for having a drink in the middle of the day."

"No, thank you. I'm on duty." Joe almost rolled his eyes for the second time, then thought about how Jodie would react to Mr. Tyson referring to his wife as the "little woman." Tyson didn't know how fortunate he was that Jodie wasn't in the room.

"You said you wanted to interview me, so what would you like to know? Is this for a publication?" Terrence asked.

Joe hadn't expected that Mr. Tyson would think this was about *him*. Perhaps he was one of those people who always assumed *everything* was about him.

"Actually, my first question is about this past Valentine's Day. I was wondering where you were?"

"That seems like an odd question, but I was in Minneapolis with my wife celebrating the holiday—or, should I say, the occasion for wasting a ridiculous amount of money."

How romantic. Joe felt even sorrier for Tyson's wife than he had before.

"I would imagine your wife and someone else could verify that, too?"

"The friends we met for dinner. And the hotel where

we stayed. Why are you asking me about this?"

"As I said before, I'm on duty. I'm investigating a shooting."

"Who was shot?"

"Pastor Kate Roberts."

"There *is* justice in the world," Terrence said coldly.

Joe was shocked at such a statement about any person, and he was taken aback at such harsh words about a pastor, especially Pastor Kate. "Why do you say that?" Joe asked, trying to keep his composure.

"She ruined our church. When I was the council president, we had a wonderful, dynamic pastor and congregation. He was bringing all sorts of people into the church. There were families joining. Even men started coming to church more often. He made *one* mistake, and everyone was out to hang him. The denomination removed him from their roster. A lot of us were ready to leave the church body, keep our congregation intact, and keep him as our pastor, anyway.

"Then *she* came along. It shows you what happens when they let a woman be in charge. She got enough people, especially a lot of the women, to listen to her, and they voted to stay in the denomination. So, we started our own church—Freedom Church. We meet in a storefront in a town ten miles away. Soon, however, we will have enough money to build, and we'll see what happens when we have a state-of-the-art building just a few miles outside of town. What's left of their congregation will pay the price."

"So, it sounds like you were pretty upset. Were there others who felt as strongly as you, who might want to hurt Kate Roberts?"

"Possibly, but I don't know who they are, and even if I

did, I'd never tell. That's their personal choice—who they like and who they don't. Last I knew, we still had that freedom in our country."

Joe could see he wouldn't get any further with this person. "If you change your mind and think of anyone, or hear anything, give me a call. In the meantime, I'll be checking out your alibi. I will need your spouse's contact information and the hotel's and restaurant's, while you are at it," Joe said, getting his pen ready to write. He would check this man's financials, too, just like the Kramers. People with resources could afford to pay for shooters. They never want to get their own hands dirty. He would also check Tyson's firearms record.

Joe glanced around the room one last time, taking in the view from the window as he stood up to leave. Nothing looked beautiful to him anymore. Everything seemed polluted by the likes of Terrence Tyson.

As Joe drove home, he wondered how one becomes a person like Terrence Tyson. Joe could live with people having resources—his own best friend, Simon, had accumulated quite a bit of wealth in the past few years. Yet, Joe could not imagine Simon talking about a pastor like that, or about his wife. Even the most chauvinistic officer Joe knew in the sheriff's department didn't come close to matching Terrence Tyson. It was even more shocking knowing that the man had been a church council president.

Joe couldn't wait to get away from Tyson's property as quickly as possible. He pointed his cruiser toward Farmerton, and instead of dwelling on Tyson, he thought about all the good men he had known over the years—his dad, his father-in-law, and especially his boss, the sheriff. The sheriff had been married for thirty years and had a sweet wife who was a kindergarten teacher. They were parents of two wonderful young adult children. The sheriff's daughter had recently completed her Bachelor of Arts degree in Criminal Justice from the University of Wisconsin-Platteville and had started working with a sheriff's department on the other side of Madison. She had fielded many offers, as she was at the top of her class.

The sheriff's son had chosen to study music, which his boss admitted was hard to accept at first, but he had seen how much his son loved it and had learned to appreciate his choice and support him fully. The young man was now in his second year of college at Belmont University in Nashville, and his boss was extremely proud of his development as a musician.

Joe also thought again about his father, who could have easily slid into becoming someone like his dad, Joe's grandfather. Instead, he learned how to be a good man from his mother's father, Joe's great-grandfather. He also had a great role model in one of his high school teachers, the person who had encouraged him to go to college. His dad also had a boss at the grocery store where he had worked, who was always encouraging and had given him good guidance.

Joe kept thinking about all these wonderful men and started to enjoy the snowy landscape once again. He turned onto the highway toward Farmerton, wondering what new piece of the puzzle he might uncover next.

Chapter 17

Joe wanted to get to Clifford's farm before it was completely dark. The days were noticeably longer now, which was one good thing about February, but there still wasn't as much daylight as Joe would like there to be. He was grateful to have an extra half an hour to work with, though, especially with the rural roads and driveways he often had to maneuver.

Clifford owned about ninety acres of land, eighty of it tillable. The rest held the old farmhouse, barn, shed, chicken coop, and a small pasture. And as Joe had expected, Clifford's driveway was a bear to contend with. At least it had been cleared of snow, and spots of gravel were beginning to peek through where the sun hit it.

Clifford was moving snow with an old Bobcat frontend loader when Joe's cruiser bumped up the long, winding, and uneven gravel driveway. His heart began beating wildly as he watched Joe stop the vehicle close to the farmhouse. How would he explain himself to the officer? He felt like driving away, but he knew that would only make things worse. He should not have done what he had done, even though it had given him some momentary satisfaction.

Clifford parked the loader close to the front door of the farmhouse, turned off the engine, and climbed down. His cheeks were red from being outside for over an hour, but he could feel blood rushing to his ears, too. He could never seem to control that from happening when he was in embarrassing or stressful situations.

Clifford didn't know what to say to the sergeant. He had seen him at St. John's Church a time or two but didn't really know him. Clifford never knew what to say to anyone. He was so socially awkward. So, he just led the officer to the door of the screened porch and opened it for him, taking off his old, tattered farm jacket, hat, and gloves and throwing them on top of one of two old rocking chairs on the porch.

He opened the door into the house and walked up a few steps covered in ancient linoleum. Then Clifford opened another door. Joe followed him and found himself stepping into the kitchen. Joe almost gasped as a thirty-caliber rifle came directly into view. It was leaning against a small closet, just inside the door.

Clifford motioned to Joe to sit down on one of the old oak chairs around a square wooden table, which was cluttered with bills and other mail, a salt and pepper shaker, and a white and turquoise ceramic sugar bowl decorated with a wheat pattern, with a matching creamer next to it. The creamer had a small chip on the rim.

Joe was suddenly taken back to his grandma's house when he was a little boy, although hers was much tidier. Clifford didn't sit down right away. Joe watched him as he clicked on the burner on the stove below a blue enamel coffee pot. Clifford, wearing overalls over a red plaid flannel shirt, swiftly added a large scoop of Folgers to the pot, then grabbed an egg from a wire basket on the counter and cracked it into the grounds. Joe remembered his grandma talking about "cooking" coffee that way in her church growing up. It was called Norwegian coffee by some, Swedish by others, or Scandinavian if one didn't want to discriminate.

Clifford had been taught by his uncle to always have a pot ready to make coffee for company. This was the first time he remembered ever having company, if one could call a law enforcement officer who was probably going to arrest him "company." Clifford, his ears still burning red by the feel of it, still didn't have a plan about how to handle his current situation. He shouldn't have let his emotions get the better of him, no matter how good it had felt in the moment.

Clifford watched the coffee cook, timing it to the exact three minutes of boiling time. Afterward, he slid the pot to another burner, added a cup of cold water, and waited a minute for the coffee grounds to settle. Then he poured two cups, one for Joe and one for himself, thinking it might be his last good cup of coffee for a long time.

With a shaky hand, Clifford set a cup in front of Joe, then pulled the sugar bowl within Joe's reach.

"Sorry I don't have any good milk for you, but I have a little of that store-bought if you want. Gave up milking three years ago. I just keep some beef cattle and my chickens now. Growing corn, oats, and alfalfa to feed 'em—that's all I can keep up with anymore," Clifford said. He sighed and wondered who would take care of his animals when he went to jail.

"Black is fine," Joe said.

Clifford sat down on a chair adjacent to Joe. He wanted to sip his coffee, but was afraid he would spill it, as his nerves were starting to get the better of him. He could hear his own heartbeat in his ears.

Joe took a sip of the coffee, just to be polite, especially

after watching the effort Clifford had put into making it. His expectations, however, had been quite low, so he was happily surprised as the liquid filled his mouth. It was one of the smoothest cups of coffee he had ever tasted. Joe was just about to compliment Clifford on it when Clifford spoke.

"I didn't mean to do it!" the farmer blurted out in a loud voice.

Joe set his coffee down.

"What didn't you mean to do?" he asked, glancing again at the rifle in the room.

"Pastor Kate."

Now Joe was on high alert. Was this man confessing to shooting the pastor?

"What about Pastor Kate?"

"I was mad at her. I just wanted to give her a present at church—some of my best eggs. She took them, but then she told me not to give her any more gifts, and it made me really, really angry," Clifford said, then stopped speaking. His hands instinctively flew up to cover his beet-red ears.

"And that's why you shot her?"

"What? Wait! No, I didn't shoot her." The man tried to compose himself. "I let the air out of her tire after church. I thought she was different from the others, but she doesn't like me, either."

Joe let out a breath of relief, although he still wondered about the rifle sitting in the house of someone who was "really, really angry" with Pastor Kate.

"So, where were you last Friday evening?" Joe asked.

"I was here. I did chores, then had some ham and eggs for dinner. And after that, I made some popcorn and watched a show on TV."

"You didn't go to the dance?"

"I thought about it, but I was still angry, and didn't want to run into Pastor Kate again."

"Can anyone verify that you were here alone all evening?"

Clifford looked frightened. "No, I can't say that anyone would know whether I was here or there—or dead or alive, for that matter." Clifford sounded so sad that Joe was getting concerned about him. He glanced over at the rifle again.

"You have a thirty-caliber rifle, I see. What do you use that for?" Joe asked.

"I used to hunt, but these days I just use it on coons and other critters that get too close to my chicken coop."

"So, you wouldn't mind if I took it with me and had ballistics check on it?" the sergeant inquired.

"You mean you're not arresting me?"

"Not unless you are confessing to a shooting. But don't let your anger make you do foolish things, Clifford—not to anyone, or to yourself. Also, don't leave the area."

"I don't ever leave the area. I have animals that depend on me. I would never leave them on purpose." Clifford was so happy he could have hugged Joe.

For the first time in a long time, Clifford smiled. A great burden lifted off his shoulders. He had confessed his crime to an officer of the law, and he was being shown mercy.

Joe took another big sip of his coffee. "Good coffee, Clifford. Thank you. And just so you know, people like pastors and law enforcement officers aren't really supposed to accept gifts from people. That's why I pay for all my meals at Bud's and for all my haircuts down at Sissy's. It's about being professional. It's not anything personal," Joe told the farmer.

For the first time, Clifford felt sorry that Pastor Kate had been injured.

"I didn't know," he remarked softly, then added, "I'm glad you liked my coffee."

Joe took two more big sips, then rose. He went over to the rifle and took out a glove from one of the compartments attached to his belt.

"Be careful," Clifford said. "I keep it loaded."

Joe carefully took five bullets from the magazine of the rifle and dropped them into an evidence bag he had retrieved from another pouch.

"I'll get this back to you as soon as I can," Joe said.

Clifford nodded, still smiling because he wasn't going to jail.

Joe drove down the long, bumpy driveway. It was already getting dark, but he had to drop the gun off at the department so the testing could begin. He was quite certain that Clifford was telling the truth, but Joe wouldn't be doing his job if he didn't check out a firearm matching the description of one used in a crime.

Joe drove away from the farm, feeling sorry for "Ol' Cliffy," as the guys down at Bud's referred to him. Joe felt exceptionally grateful that he had someone to go home to.

Chapter 18

Conrad quickly put Elizabeth's scarf back in the desk drawer before anyone happened to walk in and see him with it. He knew it had been wrong of him. He never should have gone to Farmerton. He had only wanted to get a glimpse of her, one more time. He thought about how disappointed his therapist would be if she knew what he had done.

Conrad's phone buzzed on his desk. He sighed, as the only person without a song attached to her number was his third ex-wife, Genevieve. He wondered what he had done—or not done—this time.

"Good afternoon, Genevieve," he said, like he was speaking to a client.

"Did you receive my email about Marissa's spring break trip?" Genevieve asked, her tone expressing annoyance.

"I haven't checked my personal emails today. I've been busy—"

"She needs money for her ski trip to Alta. It's due by the end of the week. The details are in the email, so please attend to it," she said coolly.

"I will handle it as soon as I'm off the phone," Conrad said. He no longer argued about money, or anything, with his ex-wife of now five months. This was partly because it rarely changed the outcome of the situation, and partly because of his guilt. He knew he hadn't been fair to

Genevieve, not at any point in their nineteen years of marriage. He had never loved her the way a person should love one's spouse. He had honestly tried, but his heart didn't really have room for her.

Conrad's marriage to Genevieve reminded him of an arranged one. His mother knew Genevieve's mother. They were in the same bridge club. When Genevieve's boyfriend of many years had been unfaithful, she called off the relationship and had been heartbroken. Genevieve's mother contacted Nina Kramer and suggested her daughter and Conrad go out together, as they were both "single" again.

Conrad, at that time, had been an absolute wreck. After his divorce from Elizabeth, he had jumped right into another relationship with a woman who physically resembled Elizabeth, but that was about it as far as similarities went. The couple had eloped in Las Vegas six months after meeting. Their marriage was a disaster and lasted less than a year.

As part of the divorce settlement, the judge, upon hearing about Conrad's behavior in the marriage and in his previous one, had ordered him to complete an anger management course. He completed it, but had pretty much faked his way through it. He was very good at covering up his true feelings. After all, he had years of practice.

When Genevieve came into his life, it was only a year after his second divorce. The mothers arranged a lunch date for them at the newest and finest restaurant in Chicago at that time. They even paid for it.

Genevieve was very different from Elizabeth. She had long, shiny dark hair and warm brown eyes. She was the type of woman who caught the attention of many men, and once had been asked to consider modeling as a career.

She was working in marketing and had a reputation as a shrewd businesswoman. The combination of her beauty and abilities made her formidable. Conrad found that aspect of her attractive. He liked her and admired her, but never learned to love her.

Even so, when Genevieve mentioned marriage, he said that would probably be a good idea. He thought—actually, he had hoped that he would grow to love her, or that at least their friendship would be enough to make the marriage work. Unfortunately, his hopes never came to fruition.

Their parents were ecstatic when they had gotten together. The two families hosted a lavish wedding. The ceremony was at St. James Cathedral in downtown Chicago. Later, there was a cocktail hour, followed by a five-course dinner, and, lastly, dancing to a live orchestra. It was the wedding and marriage Conrad's mother had always dreamed of for him, and for a while, she was more civil to Conrad than she had ever been in his lifetime. That was another good thing that came out of the relationship with Genevieve.

There were two other things for which he was truly thankful to his ex-wife. The first was their daughter, Marissa, a brown-eyed, dark-haired beauty like her mother. Unfortunately, lately it felt like his daughter was drifting further away from him since the divorce became final. Some of it may have been due to her spreading her wings in college, another part being that she was very close to her mother, and being too friendly with her dad felt like a betrayal of her mom. At least the divorce hadn't happened until Marissa left home for college. Things might have been even worse if it had been while she was still in high school. He supposed that was why Genevieve hadn't served him divorce papers until after their daughter had graduated.

The second thing Conrad was grateful for was the counselor Genevieve had made him go to years before, who he was still seeing on a regular basis. Even though the therapist, Meg, had not been able to help salvage their marriage, Conrad had truly faced his "demons" for the first time in his life. The counselor had helped him deal with his anger issues and condescending and controlling behaviors. He was glad that, by the time his daughter got into junior high, she was able to witness him becoming a more tolerant and healthy human being, one who had continued to get healthier as time went on.

Conrad had been changing in a good way ever since his second session with Meg, a therapist who had been happily married to the same man for thirty years and was the proud mother of two. He didn't know what it was about her, but he found himself unloading years and years of unhappiness, anger, and grief. He hadn't been that comfortable talking with anyone since his early years with Elizabeth. Even then, he had been ashamed to show Elizabeth what kind of person he really was, and what kind of family he had. He didn't want her to know how small and insignificant his parents, especially his mother, made him feel.

Nina Kramer continually cut her only son down with her sharp, cruel tongue. As a boy, Conrad would often cry himself to sleep at night. He couldn't let Elizabeth know just how much his mother controlled his life. Over the years, she had chosen his classes in high school, where he went to college and law school, and even who to ask and what to wear to his high school prom. In fact, the only thing he had ever been strong enough to stand up for in his life was his decision to marry Elizabeth.

He could tell these things to Meg. With her, there were no feelings of shame, only relief and a chance to be unburdened of his past. Even when it came to the toughest part for Conrad to accept, he was able to work through it—when Meg helped him realize that he had become everything he despised in his parents. Yes, Meg had worked wonders with Conrad over the years, but, alas, even though his behaviors changed for the good, there was one thing Meg couldn't do, and that was make Conrad fall in love with his wife.

When Genevieve hung up, Conrad immediately opened his email and took care of the ski trip costs. If the trip brought his daughter some joy during a tough year for their family, it was a small price to pay.

After he finished this task, he thought back to Farmerton. He should not have gone there. He had rented a Chevy instead of driving his own car. He didn't want to call attention to himself, driving a luxury car from out of state. He had stood near Elizabeth's mailbox. That's where he had spied the scarf on the ground and picked it up.

A dog had started barking and he got scared and started running to his car. He turned right into a trash can and its contents spilled to the ground. He didn't want to leave it, but he also didn't want to be seen. If Elizabeth saw him, she might call the police, and he wouldn't have blamed her.

He thought about the restraining order he had been under many years before. In the months after the divorce, Conrad had been following Elizabeth around near the courthouse. She had asked him to stay away, and he just wouldn't, or couldn't, seem to do it. He sent her mean texts and emails and continued to sneak around to see where she was going after she got home and who she was with. He had been convinced there must have been someone else in her life for her to want to leave him, but there had not. He had alienated Elizabeth all by himself but hadn't been able to admit it at that point in his life.

Someday he hoped he might have a chance to apologize to her, but only on her terms, and only if she was open to it. That's why he shouldn't have gone to Wisconsin. If Elizabeth ever found out he had been that close to her house, she might never be open to seeing him again—ever—and that would be the worst thing Conrad could imagine.

And now, she was injured, most likely in a hospital somewhere. He pulled out his phone and called his favorite investigator, the one that had helped him finally locate Elizabeth.

Chapter 19

It was only Wednesday, but Joe felt like he had been working for weeks on this case. He couldn't believe that, with all the people they had working on this case, there were so few leads. Everyone's alibis seemed to be holding up, and he had just received the ballistic report clearing Clifford's rifle. It was not the weapon used to shoot Pastor Kate. Joe was relieved that Clifford was not involved. He also felt good that his gut instinct was still spot on.

However, that meant there was still a shooter out there, and no one knew who it was. He pulled out his computer and started searching for the two men who were hurt by the man Pastor Kate and her ex-husband had gotten off in court. He was also going to investigate that man, John Germaine, as well, especially since Kate had gone up against him in court the second time around.

Just as he was about to begin reading about John Germaine, his phone rang. It was the sheriff's office, so maybe there was some new information.

"Zimmerman here," he said.

"Hey, Joe. Andy here. I've got a woman here who will only talk to you. She says she thinks she knows who shot the pastor."

"Put her on. Thanks, Andy."

"You bet. Here you go," he said.

"Sergeant Joe Zimmerman here. How may I help you?"

After a pause, he heard someone take a deep breath. "I

think..." It was a woman with a quiet, frightened-sounding voice. "I think my ex shot the pastor," she said in a shaky voice.

"First of all, to whom am I speaking? And secondly, why do you think that?"

Joe got out his pen to record her information.

"This is Paula Petermann. I think you may have seen me at church sometime, although I don't go there anymore. I stay away from places my ex might find me. Anyway, my husband, now my ex, once said he was going to 'kill that B'—actually, he said a different word than that, but I don't swear much, especially about a pastor. Anyway, he's a big hunter and owns a lot of guns. And I guess on Saturday night, he was drunk at a bar and laughing about the pastor getting shot, saying things like 'that's what she gets for sticking her nose into other people's business,' and things like that. My friend was there and heard it and called me the next day. I've been trying to decide if I should say anything about it or not. I was scared."

"What makes you think he would do such a thing?" Joe asked.

"Because he hates the pastor. He blames her for our marriage breaking up," Paula said.

"How would the pastor cause your marriage to break up?"

"Because she told me I didn't have to put up with the things my husband was doing and saying, and I decided that she was right."

"Can you stay at the office for a while and wait for me to get there, so we can do this interview face-to-face?"

"As long as I'm out of here in time to get to work by five, I'll be okay."

"What is your husband's name?"

"Ex-husband. Tommy Petermann."

Joe was going to check to see if there was anything in the system on this man, so it would be waiting for him when he got there.

"Is that short for Thomas?"

"Yes, sir."

Joe snapped his laptop shut, grabbed his equipment, and headed out the door. Jodie hadn't slept well, so she was still in bed, and he didn't want to wake her up. He left her a note and headed to the office, hoping for some answers.

When Joe arrived, he saw the diminutive woman sitting in a chair next to his desk. She was barely over five feet tall, with a small-boned frame and long, blonde hair. An arrest report was on his desk. The woman looked downward and sat with slumped shoulders. He greeted her and introduced himself. Her handshake was weak and her fingers trembled, and Joe couldn't help but notice that she pulled back when he first put his hand out toward her and introduced himself. He had seen that response before, usually by physically abused people.

Paula sat quietly as he looked over the report on Thomas Petermann. There were three disorderly conduct charges, all of which were eventually dropped. The last one was over a year before. There were two speeding tickets issued over the past five years, and a couple of warnings. All of these happened in the county, but in a different area than the one Joe usually patrolled.

Joe turned toward Paula. "Do you think Thomas is capable of shooting someone?"

"If he was drunk, I think he could be capable of anything. And in the past couple of years, that's pretty much all the time," Paula said sadly.

"Do you have contact information for him?"

Paula gave him Thomas's last-known address, phone number, and place of employment. "And if you can't find him at any of those, he would probably be at Barney's," Paula said, referring to a bar and grill in another town.

Joe asked her for her phone number. She said she didn't have her own phone right now. That was why she had gotten a ride to the sheriff's office. A volunteer driver was waiting for her. Later, another driver would take her to her job, where she worked in a back room and wasn't visible to the public. She said she was living at a women's shelter, but hopefully would be getting her own place sometime soon. Joe knew of two shelters in the area, but didn't press her for more information. She had obviously been through a lot and was worried for her safety.

"I will check out Thomas's whereabouts last Friday night. I thank you for your information, and please call me if you hear of anything else or need anything else. Also, my wife is a deputy and if you ever need either one of us, please call." Joe produced his card, then wrote Jodie's name and cell phone number on the back.

Paula thanked him, and Joe watched her head out of the door to a waiting car where an older woman sat behind the wheel. He felt sad that people had to live their lives like Paula had to live hers currently. He hoped she would be able to get her own place soon and move on with her life.

◈

Joe drove his cruiser and parked across the street from Barney's. It was only ten in the morning, but there were several pickups parked in front of it.

As Joe stepped inside the bar and grill, the smell of stale beer assaulted his nostrils. A whiff of cigarette smoke came in along with Joe from a man smoking just outside the front door, as it was prohibited inside Wisconsin businesses. The establishment seemed dark to Joe, except for the lights coming from an old pinball machine and a race car video game in a corner. There were a few booths around the edges of the room, the seats and backs covered in maroon vinyl. In the center of the room were some square wooden tables and chairs. The back of the room hosted a long wooden bar, behind which shelves of bottled liquor lined a mirror backdrop. Neon lights promoting different brands of beer decorated the walls. A large sign advertised some upcoming meat raffles over the next couple of weekends, raising funds for a fishing tournament on the Mississippi for youth in the spring.

At the bar, there were a dozen stools covered in the same vinyl as the booths. Three of them were occupied. One bartender was on duty, a gray-haired man wearing a green T-shirt that said "Barney's" across the chest. The man asked Joe what he could get him. Joe thought about having a soda, but he really wanted to get out of this depressing place as quickly as possible.

"I was wondering if Thomas Petermann was around?"

A tall man sitting at one of the stools twirled around quickly. The man looked to be almost six and a half feet tall, and Joe placed him around two hundred and forty pounds. He tried to imagine Paula having any chance against this man.

The man saw Joe's uniform, saluted, and said, "Present and accounted for, sir," then laughed, as did his friends at the bar with him.

Thomas was wearing jeans and a hooded sweatshirt underneath a tan canvas work jacket. He had steel-toed work boots on. Joe knew from the report that this man was employed at a nearby factory, driving a forklift on the second shift, Sunday through Thursday. He hoped he would sober up before he got to work later.

"I just have a couple of questions for you. Would you like to go to a booth and answer them?" Joe asked Thomas.

"Anything you have to ask, you can ask right here. I have nothing to hide."

"Just wondering about your whereabouts last Friday evening, particularly between seven and nine?"

"Well, that's an easy one. I was at work," Thomas lied.

"Try again," Joe retorted.

"What night did you say again?" Thomas asked, back-pedaling.

"Friday. Valentine's Day, seven to nine o'clock."

"I was right here, wasn't I, guys? That's fish fry night, you know. Best anywhere."

They shook their heads in agreement. Joe looked at the bartender.

"I'm in the back frying fish, so I can't help you on that one, Officer," the man said.

"Who was the bartender that evening, and how can I get ahold of him or her?"

"That would be Brenda. She'll be in from five to closing."

"Do you have a phone number for her right now?"

"She's probably still sleeping," the bartender said.

"As I asked, do you have a phone number for her?"

The bartender reluctantly wrote a phone number on the back of a paper bar coaster.

Joe was going to call this woman right away before someone could call her and warn her, but he wasn't fast enough. Her phone went to voicemail, and when he looked back inside the bar, Thomas was on his cell phone.

Joe called her again a few minutes later and she answered this time.

"Brenda, this is Sergeant Joe Zimmerman from the Sheriff's Department. I'm supposing you were expecting my call," Joe said, trying to get her to admit she had talked to Thomas.

She sounded hesitant. "Why, no, ah, you just woke me up," she said.

"You understand I can look at your phone records?" Joe said. He didn't mention that he would need a subpoena to do that. "Again, you were expecting my call, correct?"

"I guess so," Brenda replied.

"Try again."

"Yes, I was expecting to hear from you. What is this all about?"

"I would like to talk to you in person. I just have a few questions for you."

She sounded hesitant again. "If you can come here right away. I only have a short time before..." She didn't finish her sentence.

Joe said he would be right over. He had looked up her address and she was only a couple blocks away.

Joe pulled up in front of a small, clapboard house in need of painting. Brenda came out to the porch in a robe to meet him, even though it was only thirty-eight degrees outside. She was a tall woman, about five-foot-ten, and looked strong. Her face had that grayish hue of a heavy smoker and her voice on the phone was husky, another tell-tale sign.

Joe introduced himself and showed her his badge. "I'm looking for witnesses who saw Thomas Petermann at Barney's between seven and nine last Friday night. Can you vouch for his presence there during that time?"

"He was there. He's always there." She started to shake. Joe wasn't sure if it was the cold, her obvious discomfort, or a little bit of both.

"Are there other people you can remember who could also verify this?"

"I don't know. It's crazy busy every Friday night—it's our fish fry night, and last Friday was Valentine's Day on top of it. Again, what's this all about? I've got to get going," she said, and looked both ways down the street like she was watching for someone.

"If you think of anyone else, please give me a call," Joe said, handing her his card.

He walked to his patrol car, looking both ways to see if anyone was coming. She seemed nervous to him, and he was pretty sure she hadn't been completely truthful with him. He decided he would go to the bar again that night after she was on shift, and talk to her when Thomas was at work and not around to intimidate her. He also wanted to see if anyone else remembered seeing Thomas at the bar on Valentine's evening.

As Joe drove back to Farmerton, he called Pastor Kate to see what she had to say about Thomas. The pastor answered on the fourth ring. She was getting stronger by the minute, it seemed, and he had been thrilled when she had texted him earlier saying she could now use her cell phone.

"It's so good to hear your voice, Joe," Kate said.

Joe felt the same way about her. "Just checking to see how you are doing, and to ask you a question about someone."

"I am feeling better today—stronger and awake more."

"Those are all good signs," Joe replied.

"They are. Now, who are we talking about?"

"A Thomas Petermann. His ex-wife is Paula."

"I never really met him, just heard about him." Kate told Joe how she had arrived at the church one morning about two years before, and a woman was waiting outside, asking if she could just sit in the church. She was young, in her twenties, but something about her seemed older than that. She had tears in her eyes, and smelled of alcohol, even though it was only nine in the morning.

Pastor Kate showed her the way to the sanctuary and told her she would come back and check on her. After half an hour, she poked her head into the worship space. The young woman was praying out loud, tears streaming down her face.

The pastor gave her some more time, then came back and sat down quietly beside her until the woman stopped speaking and crying. The woman finally turned toward the pastor.

"My husband. He isn't nice to me. He's just so mean—all the time. Nothing I do is right. Nothing I do is enough."

"Have you tried marriage counseling?"

"He says counseling is for pus—" She stopped. "He won't go to one." She took a deep breath. "He used to be wonderful. He was handsome and sweet. He had a job. He was a good baseball player in high school, and all the girls wanted to be his girlfriend. I felt so special when he chose me. But then he started drinking—more and more all the time. He drinks up most of his paycheck, so we live pretty much on mine. We had to move into a trailer park because we lost our house. It's just so sad. I'm so sad."

The pastor just let her talk and talk that morning and invited her to come to church, which she did for the next six months.

"She never reported any physical abuse, Joe, but I always thought she may have been holding back. I did tell her that she didn't have to put up with abuse of any type. The last time I saw her, she told me she was filing for a divorce. She came to church once after that, then she just disappeared."

"She's been living in a shelter for a while now, so I would imagine you were right that there was more abuse than she was letting on, or maybe that came about after she chose to divorce him. That may have launched him into new territory," Joe remarked.

"True," said Pastor Kate. "It's so sad. You don't think he had anything to do with the shooting, do you?"

"He has an alibi—at least for now, but I'll keep my eye on him. He seems like he's a ticking time bomb."

"Be careful, Joe."

"I will. Now, you take care and get back to getting better," Joe said, smiling for the first time that day.

Joe hated to be late getting home that evening, but he thought it best to go back to Barney's right at five o'clock when Brenda would be coming on shift. At first, he thought he had wasted his time, as he didn't see her right away, but then she came out of the door from the kitchen. She took one look at Joe and turned away to do something at the other end of the bar.

Joe sat on a barstool and waited until she had to acknowledge him, as another customer near him called her by name and wanted a beer. She came toward them and now Joe could see why she had turned away. She was wearing heavy makeup, but he could see a welt and discoloration under her right eye that hadn't been there earlier in the day.

"What happened to you, Brenda?" the other customer asked.

"Walked into a door. I'm such a ditz."

"Can I help you, Officer?" Brenda asked, finally acknowledging Joe.

"I'd like to order two of your specials to go."

Brenda shouted the order to the kitchen over her shoulder, then turned back to Joe, wiping the bar with a cloth even though there was really nothing to clean up. He could tell she was nervous again.

"Just making sure you hadn't thought of anyone else who was here last Friday night."

"I told you. I don't know who was here."

"Hey, I was here!" It was the customer sitting next to him. Brenda turned ashen.

Turning to the customer, Joe asked, "Do you know Thomas Petermann?"

"You mean Tommy?"

"Yes," Joe answered.

"What about him?"

"Just wondering if he was here last Friday night—say, from seven until nine?"

"If he was, I never saw him. Usually, he's the first one here and the last one to leave on Friday nights."

Joe turned back to Brenda. "So, would you like to change your answer from earlier today?"

Brenda looked like she was trying to weigh her options. "Can we talk over there?" she said, pointing to the other end of the bar. Joe gladly joined her.

"I don't know what you want from me, but no, Tommy wasn't here last Friday. But I do know where he was. He was cheating on me with another woman over in Dubuque. He even took her out for a Valentine's Day dinner at a real restaurant. My friend and her husband saw them."

It wasn't the answer Joe had expected. He got the contact for her friend, and by then, his food was ready to go. He paid Brenda for it, and gave her another one of his cards, not knowing if she still had the one from earlier or not.

"If you need *anything*, give me a call. Take care, Brenda," he said. He picked up his sack of food and was on his way.

It had been a sad day—a sad week. Each day had been filled with stories of people hurting another or treating someone badly. Joe sighed. He couldn't wait to get home to his Jodie; to a place of kindness, respect, and love. Again, Joe felt so grateful for the life he was living.

Chapter 20

Both Joe and Jodie had slept fitfully that night—Jodie because she was a month away from her due date, and Joe because of the people and situations he had dealt with over the past few days.

In the morning, Joe dragged himself to the kitchen table for breakfast. He made a pot of oatmeal, enough that Jodie could have some when she got up. Today he was going to investigate John Germaine and the people he had assaulted. He knew it was a long shot that they were involved, but there were not any other leads popping up, and he had to do something.

Joe spooned the steaming cereal into a bowl and topped it with walnuts, brown sugar, and a splash of milk. It had become his go-to winter breakfast as of late. Then he checked the *Wisconsin State Journal* newspaper on his phone, wondering when the Badger basketball team played next. He wished he could get to a game, but that was out of the question this season with a very pregnant wife at home. He was nervous enough being away from home for work.

Jodie had just shifted into administrative work at the beginning of the week, which, thanks to technology, could be done at home. She mentioned it wasn't quite as bad or as boring as she had thought it would be, and because she was feeling more fatigued as of late, she was happy not to be out in the field presently.

Joe rinsed his bowl and spoon in the kitchen sink and put them in the dishwasher. He put the leftover oats in a microwaveable bowl and washed the pot and spoon by hand, dried them, and put them away. Then he wrote a note for Jodie, telling her there was breakfast in the fridge for her if she wanted.

Joe bundled up, as the temperature had dropped significantly from the day before. He checked in with everyone at the office who was working on the case. Again, there was no new information. No one could figure out how this crime could have happened so easily. It appeared to be an almost seamless operation, which made Joe wonder if there wasn't more than one person involved.

Joe thought about Thomas Petermann. He had believed he could be the perpetrator, but the more Joe thought about it, he wasn't sure "Tommy" was ever sober enough to think something like the shooting through, let alone carry the plan out. Then again, he had somehow managed to stay out of jail, even though he had been abusive to his ex-wife, and most likely other women, like Brenda.

Putting the thoughts about Thomas aside, Joe decided to start his search regarding John Germaine. He found his social media page first. There he was, smiling away on a yacht on Lake Michigan. The post was from the past September, and there had been none since. Joe dug further. There were some posts about John's insurance business, which had won an award at the end of the last calendar year just six weeks ago. Of course, the company posted over and over about this award through the month of January, tagging him on their posts, but then the posts abruptly stopped.

Joe decided to call the insurance agency and see if

he could speak with the man. When he called, the office manager answered the phone. When Joe asked if he could speak with John, the woman said he was unavailable and would be for an indeterminate amount of time.

Joe told her who he was and asked if everything was okay. The woman sounded like she was going to burst into tears at any moment.

"Mr. Germaine is detained out of the country at this time."

"And what do you mean by detained, exactly?"

The woman hesitated. "He's in jail—in Belize. He got into a fight and badly hurt another man. His lawyer went down there, but isn't certain what he can do about the situation. Now we don't know exactly what to do with the agency in the meantime. We have another agent, but he can't handle everything by himself, and I can only direct calls to others. I have no authority in business matters. It's just awful."

"I'm sorry to hear that," Joe said sincerely. "I hope things work out for you." He truly felt sorry for the woman and the other insurance agent, victims of sorts, and even sorrier for yet another victim of this man's violent behavior. "By the way, who is his lawyer?" Joe wondered if Conrad was representing him once more.

"Someone I've never heard of before. He used to use Mr. Kramer, but he refused to take his case this time."

He wasn't certain why, but Joe felt relieved to hear that Conrad Kramer was no longer John Germaine's lawyer.

He was just about to investigate Germaine's victims in his second assault case when he was called to help with a crash. He didn't often get called in on those anymore, but this was fairly serious and another officer was working on another accident, so off he went to the other side of the county.

Joe pulled up to a fiery scene. There was a pickup truck and a carload of Amish farmers who had hitched a ride with a neighbor to go to the Farm and Fleet store in Dubuque. The pickup truck had been coming from Dubuque. It was currently on its side and burning. Two people, a man and a woman, had been pulled from it and dragged away. Joe looked at the two people being tended to by the EMTs and recognized one as Tommy Petermann, who was badly burned on one side of his body. The rest of his body looked bloody, and Joe thought he had some broken bones. The other was a woman he did not know and appeared to have multiple injuries.

Miraculously, the farmers in the car had only minor injuries, as they had swerved to avoid the truck just in time. They did end up in the ditch, though, and the car had some serious damage to its undercarriage. They said the pickup had been driving toward them at a high speed and kept changing lanes. The preliminary assessment of the situation was that Tommy had been drinking and driving and swerving back and forth across the median. All this happened at nine o'clock in the morning.

Joe finished up the reports with the farmers and gave them all rides home, while ambulances took the injured to area hospitals and a tow truck took the car to a shop in Platteville for repair. While he didn't feel good about thinking and feeling this way, Joe felt relieved in a way that Tommy Petermann would not be wreaking havoc on anyone else's life again any time soon. And who knew—maybe this incident would be the man's wake-up call.

Maybe Tommy would finally reach out for the help he so obviously needed.

Conrad Kramer's investigator, Sam, never ceased to amaze him. He already had some information for Conrad after only a few days, and sent Conrad a file along with his verbal report.

First, he informed Conrad about John Germaine's arrest in Belize. Conrad already had a suspicion about this, as John had called his office asking for legal help. This time Conrad said no and told John to never contact his office again, for any reason. After now hearing that Germaine had seriously injured yet another person, he was glad he hadn't helped this time. Conrad no longer cared about how much money a person had, what they did for a living, or whether his parents knew them or wanted him to take a case. Those days were behind Conrad now, thankfully.

Hearing about John Germaine made Conrad feel guilty again for ever having defended this person who obviously had a serious problem. He remembered how Elizabeth had felt about Germaine in that very first case and how she had not wanted to sit second chair in his defense, but Conrad hadn't taken no for an answer. And then, two years later, Conrad recalled how he and his sister went all out to destroy Elizabeth in court in her final case, Elizabeth going against Germaine this time. He remembered how they had convinced her clients, the unfortunate victims, to take a pittance for their injuries and inconvenience. Ever since Conrad had become a healthier person, that one kept him up at night. If he could somehow take it all back, he would.

Conrad's investigator went on to the next people on the list, the victims in that case.

Theodore Gavin had once been a friendly acquaintance of John Germaine, and they had done some business together in the past. Sam informed Conrad that they still had a few business connections, but not as many as they used to, as Gavin had branched out into a new business venture, and a very profitable one. He was doing very well financially and, when asked about John Germaine, had not shown much response. Gavin even asked how Germaine was doing, to which Sam had said he was in jail in South America for assault. Gavin had shaken his head in disbelief, and said he thought Germaine would have "grown out of that kind of stupidity by now."

Then, when asked about his feelings about Elizabeth Kramer, Gavin had responded by asking "Who?" When he was reminded, his only remark was he remembered thinking she was "hot" for a lawyer, but that's all he really remembered about her. He mentioned that it all worked out well in the end, so he didn't really think about it anymore.

Sam's assessment was that Theodore Gavin had nothing to do with Elizabeth being shot on Valentine's Day, but he asked him where he had been that evening, anyway. He said that he and his new girlfriend had gone to New York to see her favorite musical. He mentioned how much he hated musicals, but also how much he really liked his new girlfriend. Sam later checked with his source and verified that Gavin's name had been on a flight manifest to New York.

The next victim had been Brian Banyon, who was no longer living. Relatives listed as survivors were a son,

Billy, and a daughter, Becky. Their addresses were both the same as their father's had been before his death. There was no wife listed anymore, so Sam checked into it. The couple had divorced three years after the court settlement.

Conrad thought back and remembered a woman sitting with two young children in the courtroom, but he couldn't be sure anymore. That must have been Banyon's family. His children would be somewhere in their twenties by now. Conrad wished he had paid more attention to the fact that these were actual people in these cases and thought about all the innocent people he had not been fair to over the years.

He wondered what happened to Banyon's children and asked his investigator to dig deeper. He, too, was planning to check into it that evening, but right now he was off to court.

Chapter 21

It was Friday morning. As Joe drove down Main Street on his way out of town, he thought about how excited everyone had been just one week before, and how different everything felt in Farmerton now.

In one short week's time, Pastor Kate had had two emergencies, one minor one early on Valentine's Day, and then another very serious one that evening. Farmerton had experienced its most memorable and terrifying Valentine's Day Dance ever, and for certain they would never forget it. Now they just hoped they could have a second chance at the auction, but there was another storm coming in over the weekend, so Joe wondered if it would ever happen.

Sissy had suffered her heart attack and ended up in the hospital. She was still not able to work and was recovering at home. At least the workload was lighter at the salon now that the big holiday event had passed, so her two other stylists were not as overwhelmed as they could have been. In a short phone call with Sissy the day before, she had vowed to Joe to be back at the beauty shop the following week. She mentioned that she had to get back to her "regulars," the ones that came in every week for a wash and set, and others like Joe who got trims every other week. Joe had been pleased to hear some pep in Sissy's voice. He could tell she was honestly feeling better, not faking it, and told her he was looking forward to a "little cleanup."

Joe's thoughts then drifted to his conversation with

Simon the week before and he realized he hadn't spoken to him since. Joe was just going to hit his number when his phone buzzed, and Simon's name flashed across it.

"Well, this is a little freaky," Joe said. "I was just going to call you."

"I knew you were probably going on shift. I hope I'm not interrupting anything, but I just had to talk to you," Simon said. His voice had a quiver in it, but Joe couldn't tell exactly what emotion he was hearing in Simon's voice.

"What's up?" Joe asked his friend.

"You know my sister's kids—you've heard me speak about my nieces and nephews often—well, all the time."

Joe felt anxious, and hoped nothing bad had happened to one of them. There were four children in the family, ranging in age from nine to eighteen. Simon was a very proud uncle and had been very generous to his sister's family over the past few years. It was a bit ironic, because there was a time when his sister had wanted him to keep his distance from her family, as Simon's alcoholism had been raging out of control. Now, they saw each other often. He and Sally attended the kids' school events, even though they lived fifteen miles away. They also took each child school shopping at the beginning of the school year and treated them to a lunch at a restaurant of their choice. They had all grown very close.

"Yes, I remember them. Is everything okay?"

"Well, I'm not exactly sure how to answer that question. No, but yes, it can be worked out—we hope." Simon took a deep breath. "Our niece, Olivia—the oldest—just informed her parents that she is three months pregnant."

"Didn't she just get a huge scholarship to a college out of state?"

"Yes, she's the one. The baby is due in early August, so she could still attend. She told her parents she doesn't feel she is ready to be a parent. They offered to help her raise the child, told her she could stay at home and go to the technical college nearby, but she said she still wants to go to her dream college. She doesn't want to live in a small town. She wants a college education and a career." Simon paused and took another breath, then spoke again. With great excitement in his voice, he announced, "But here's the thing—she wants *us* to adopt the baby! It's a girl," Simon said, barely able to speak anymore, overwhelmed by emotion.

"That's amazing news, Simon. And your sister is okay with that?"

Simon collected himself. "She is nervous, but frankly, she doesn't really have a say in it. Olivia is eighteen, and legally an adult. And the father, he wants nothing to do with the baby. At first, he wanted Olivia to have an abortion, but said he's okay with adoption if he doesn't have to do anything along the way. He's eighteen, too, and has already signed a document giving up his parental rights. I just can't believe this is happening. I feel so guilty for feeling so happy. I know this isn't an ideal situation for my niece, but we want to be parents so badly."

"And you will be amazing parents, Simon. Congratulations!" Joe was so happy for Simon and Sally, and so elated to hear some good news for a change. "Is it okay if I tell Jodie?"

"Of course, but no one else yet. We need all the papers to be signed. After that, we will make arrangements to help Olivia with her medical expenses, which will be a big relief to my sister and her husband."

"It sounds like a very good thing can come out of this situation, Simon. I'm sure the next few months will be awkward for your niece, but she will have a lot of support on the family front. She will also know the baby will be loved and have a bright future. I'm sure that's why she wanted you and Sally to raise her."

"Olivia has always been very special to me. For whatever reason, she always showed love to me—even when I was at my worst."

"And now you can love her and help her when she is going through a stressful time."

"I'm so happy to be able to help. And I'm so grateful to you, again, Joe, for everything you have done for me."

"Simon. You are the one who put in the work—and still put in the work every day. You have changed your own life, not me."

"Well, I'm not going to argue with you, Joe. I'm too happy to argue with anyone about anything right now."

"I understand."

"I'm going to let you get back to work, Joe. Thanks for listening to me."

"Thanks for sharing your good news with me. I'll call you sometime soon and we can make plans to celebrate."

"We would like that. Have a good day, Joe."

"I already am. Later," Joe said, and ended the call. He couldn't stop smiling. He was so happy for his friend, realizing that he and Simon would both have children of the same age. Their children could grow up together, maybe even become good friends. The thought made him smile even more. He couldn't wait to tell Jodie and called her on the way to the office.

Conrad's court case had gone very well the afternoon before, so well that the plaintiff had agreed to a settlement out of court. It was a fair deal, so he felt okay about it, but mostly he was grateful because that gave him time to check into the Banyon family.

He discovered that Billy and Becky Banyon were twins. They were now in their twenties and still lived in the small house on Chicago's south side in which they had resided since they were ten. They had been eight years old when their dad was injured. At that time, they had lived with their mom and dad in a house in Oak Park.

Conrad looked up information on their father, Brian's, social media page. There he saw photos of the children standing in front of the first house they had lived in, posing on special occasions both inside and outside. It wasn't a fancy home, but it seemed nice and a good size for a family of four. There was even a sewing room for Mrs. Banyon. He knew this because Brian had posted photos of her holding up some beautiful quilts she had crafted in her special space.

Then came some posts that mentioned the family was moving. Brian apparently had been laid off. Mrs. Banyon had unloaded her anger in a scathing post on the page railing against the company her husband had worked for. Apparently, they claimed they were downsizing. She, on the other hand, thought her husband had been treated unfairly ever since his injury. She said they never really gave him a chance after he came back from being on disability. She said the company had acted like it was in some way his fault that he had been injured and missed work for almost two months.

After that, there were only a few posts, none of them showing the house they had moved into. Conrad was familiar with their new neighborhood. It was quite a change from their last one. He thought about what a shock it must have been to the children to have to move away from their friends and go to a new school, and for Brian to have to look for a new job in a not-so-great economy.

Then, a year later, Brian Banyon made a heartbreaking post. It said it would be his last post for a while. He and his wife were getting a divorce.

Conrad felt terrible after reading about this family. He knew that Theodore Gavin and Brian Banyon had taken a bad deal—a deal he had drummed up. Frankly, he had been shocked they had taken it because it was such a lowball offer. Conrad suddenly felt responsible for the things that had happened to Brian's family. Even if he wasn't directly responsible, he knew that he had helped start the ball rolling toward this family's demise. In fact, he felt so awful that an idea came to him. He should apologize to Billy and Becky. He would go to their home the next day and do just that, and he would take his checkbook with him.

Chapter 22

On Saturday morning, Joe made pancakes and bacon for breakfast. It was a treat for the couple, as they rarely ate that type of breakfast any longer.

Jodie came into the kitchen and slid her arms around Joe's waist as he stood working at the counter.

"You are spoiling me," she said sweetly.

He turned, her arms still around him, and touched her stomach gently.

"You deserve to be spoiled—both of you," he said. Just then, the baby delivered a huge kick.

"Someone obviously agrees," Jodie said, smiling up at Joe. She had never loved this man more than she did right at this moment. She couldn't wait to meet the little one inside her they had created together.

"Wow!" was all Joe could say.

He turned back to the pancake griddle, not wanting anything to burn, and with the spatula moved some perfect pancakes from it onto a platter.

"Have a seat. Breakfast is served."

Jodie waddled over to the dining table and sat down. She laughed at herself because she couldn't get very close to the table anymore. *Soon*, she thought to herself, *soon*.

Joe and Jodie were relieved that it was finally the weekend. Joe had planned to go to Madison a little later and visit the pastor. When he returned, he would put together the crib—finally. He asked Jodie if she wanted to go with him.

Jodie thought about it for a moment, but she still felt very fatigued, even after a good breakfast. Or perhaps *because* she had eaten too much of that good breakfast.

"I'm going to take a raincheck again. I hope Pastor Kate doesn't think I don't care about her."

"That's impossible, Jodie. I think she would tell you to stay home, too," Joe responded.

"Knowing her, you are probably right."

"Of course I'm right. Aren't I always?"

Jodie gave him one of her looks.

"Okay, maybe not always, but close."

"Keep telling yourself that," she said, and stood to clear the table.

"You don't have to do that, Jodie."

"I know I don't have to, but I want to. Go take a shower and be on your way. You don't want to get stuck in bad weather in case that storm comes in earlier than expected."

Joe hugged her gently and kissed her forehead, then walked to their bedroom suite to get ready for the day.

Billy Banyon swept the kitchen floor of the small house with a broom that was older than he was. His dad had always taught him to keep things neat and clean. The linoleum was cracked in several places now, and more bits chipped off each week. Billy's dad, Brian, had hoped to have the floor tested for asbestos, and removed by professionals if need be. Brian had been saving up for new flooring when he died of a heart attack two years before.

Brian Banyon had been at his job as a custodian at a nearby manufacturing plant when he had a massive heart attack. He had once hoped to get a job on the line at the plant, but his back still bothered him from time to time, so he never applied. The thought of being hurt again and perhaps not being able to work at all had kept him in his current position. He made just enough to cover his house payments, keep the lights and heat on, and feed his children. He stressed about money almost all the time. There wasn't much left over after he bought groceries. What little there was was saved for Christmas gifts and school expenses. The kids contributed a portion of their work money to the household, but Brian wanted them to save up for college someday.

Becky and Billy were bright kids, but they had not done well in high school or on their college entrance exams. They worked at a neighborhood convenience store and were taking classes at a community college. They were getting good grades and saving some money to attend a good four-year university. They had hoped to transfer the next fall when their father suddenly passed away. They both finished their classes that semester—barely. They never went back to school after that.

Billy kicked at the linoleum floor. He was still so angry—at his mother, God, the world, and especially the people who were responsible for causing his family so much stress and unhappiness.

He thought back to the times when his mother was still around. Before their dad was injured, she had been a regular mom, like the ones all the other kids at school had. She made cookies for bake sales. She made quilts for the church auction, for each of them, and for friends and relatives.

Then their dad was in the wrong place at the wrong time. Two men were fighting, and their skirmish had tumbled out into the street, where they collided with Brian, badly injuring his shoulder and back. It was a freak accident, but in a matter of seconds, Brian Banyon and his family's lives were changed forever.

Unable to work and on disability for two months, they fell behind in their mortgage payments. After Brian went back to work, his supervisors and coworkers started looking at him differently. They whispered behind his back, and it felt like they were laughing at him. Some seemed to think he was faking it. Some thought he had been part of the fight.

Several months later, he was out of a job. According to the company, it was because they were beginning to downsize, starting with Brian Banyon. The Banyons could no longer afford to pay for their home in Oak Park, so they sold it at a buyer's price and moved.

The kids had to change schools, which was stressful enough, but the real "kicker" was when, two years later, Brian's wife, Billy and Becky's mother, announced she couldn't live like that anymore and was leaving. They eventually learned she had also been unfaithful to her husband and had a whole new life all planned out with another man. The kids were devastated but remained loyal to their dad to the very end of his life. He was only fifty-six years old when he suffered a heart attack. Billy and Becky were certain it was caused by all the stress he had endured since his injury.

Billy and Becky felt so alone in the world after their

father died, but at least they had each other. And they had the house they had shared. Their dad had made the final payment on it shortly before his death and had willed it to both of them. It wasn't much, but the siblings were happy to have a home, and a little bit of equity for the future.

Billy put the broom and dustpan away. He looked at the wall filled with framed photos. The largest one, top and center, had been taken just before their dad's injury. He was in his blaze-orange hunting clothes, as were Billy and Becky. They had been too young to hunt, but they used to sit in a deer stand for hours with their dad at his friend's wooded acreage in southern Wisconsin. Their dad rarely shot anything, but he did get a nice doe one year, the one featured in the photo with them and their dad. Their dad had donated the deer meat to a food pantry, as no one in the family had an acquired taste for wild game. Brian just enjoyed getting out of the city a few times each year to get some "peace, quiet, and fresh air," as he always told them. It was one of their favorite family memories.

Above the photo, a rifle was mounted horizontally, the same one Brian held in one hand in the photo below it. Billy turned away from it, wondering how his sister was doing with her "chore" that day. His duty was on the home front. He turned toward an overflowing basket of dirty clothes in the hallway. His next task for the day was to take the laundry to the laundromat. He never made it that day, however, as there was a knock on the door.

Chapter 23

Becky Banyon looked around nervously. She didn't want to be there, but she knew she had to finish what she—they—had started. She thought about the day her father had died, and that gave her the extra boost and courage she needed.

Their father died on Valentine's Day, two years before. Everyone in the family had been planning to be home for supper together that night, a rarity in those days with busy work and school schedules. Their dad was going to make hamburgers on the grill, even though it was only going to be thirty-some degrees by the time he arrived home. Their father always liked to "defy winter," as he put it. Billy had brought home potato chips and dip from the convenience store. Becky picked up a large can of baked beans on her way home from class. She even splurged on some heart-shaped cookies from the store bakery.

The twins set out plates and glasses, then waited for their father to get off work. It was nearing the end of his workday when the call came to the house phone. Becky had answered it, then promptly dropped the receiver when they gave her the news. Billy picked it up from the floor, then stared blankly ahead in disbelief as he was informed that their father had just suffered a major heart attack at work and had not survived.

Neither of them remembered the next few days very clearly. They had no money for a grave for their father, so he was cremated. They signed up to pay off the expense over time, as they didn't have much in the way of savings, and it would take a while before the little their dad had saved would be available to them.

They finished their semester in a zombie-like haze, went to work robotically, then each took an extra part-time job in June. By the end of the summer, they were beginning to recover financially, but not emotionally. They were sad, and, more than anything, they were mad. That's when they decided to do something about these feelings. They were going to make the person responsible for their troubles pay.

First, they had to decide who was the most responsible, and on whom they could exact revenge. They hated their father's former company, but it would be tough to pin the cause on any one person in the organization. They also remembered that a few of his former coworkers came to the little visitation and service they had at the funeral home for their dad. The company had even sent some flowers, as did his latest employer.

Those people were quickly ruled out. They thought about it some more. They remembered hearing their mom say they should have listened to their lawyer, who had told their dad not to take the deal Kramer Law offered. She said it was not anywhere near enough and was unfair. They also thought about that lawyer from Kramer Law—his expensive suit, his shiny shoes, and his obnoxiously cocky attitude. They remembered him questioning the extent of their dad's injury, and wondering why he was near the people involved in the fight in the first place—like it was his fault for being there and being injured.

When they thought that through, they decided who

they were going to get back at, and what they were going to do. They were going to kill Conrad Kramer.

The twins decided to carry out their plan on Valentine's Day, on the one-year anniversary of their father's death. Billy had secured a part-time job in the law building as a custodian. It afforded him access to many rooms. It also gave him a way to sneak a weapon into the Kramer Law office until it was needed and move around the building without being questioned.

On Valentine's Day, he gathered the knife he had stashed away in a janitorial closet and quietly headed for Conrad Kramer's office, a cleaning rag covering the weapon. He knew exactly what time Conrad usually had lunch, and exactly when the secretary would be away from her desk for a break, as well.

He quietly opened the door to Conrad's office and slipped in. There was a laptop open on top of the huge mahogany desk. Conrad's huge leather manager's chair was turned toward the floor-to-ceiling window, so Conrad couldn't see Billy enter.

"Conrad Kramer, turn around," Billy ordered. "I want you to see the face of someone whose life you ruined. And now, I'm going to ruin yours."

Finally, the chair began turning slowly. Billy was just about ready to lunge toward it and declare vengeance for his father when he saw the person in the chair was not Conrad Kramer! He couldn't believe it. In Conrad's seat was a beautiful brown-haired woman he had never seen before.

"Who are you?" Billy asked, trying not to panic too much, but he was unnerved. He pointed the knife at the woman with a shaky hand.

"I'm Genevieve Markwell Kramer. I'm Conrad Kramer's wife. Who are you?"

"That doesn't matter. I'll kill you instead. That will show him."

Genevieve was frightened, but she was a quick thinker.

"If you really want to hurt Conrad, I've got a better idea. Why do you want to kill him?"

Billy then told her about the court case and the terrible settlement that helped lead to the family's financial downfall. "He knew it wouldn't be enough to really help us, but he badgered my father into taking the deal."

"That sounds like Conrad," Genevieve said.

"Our family fell completely apart after my dad lost his job. We had to sell our house and moved into a crummy little place. My mother couldn't take it anymore, so she cheated on my dad and ran off with another man. It broke my dad's heart. All of this caused my dad so much stress that he had a heart attack—last year on Valentine's Day. Now it's just me and my twin sister who are left in our family."

"I'm so sorry that happened. I think I heard about that case." She wasn't lying, as Conrad had expressed regrets over this particular situation over the years. But what she did next was wicked.

"You know, the one you really should go after is that terrible lawyer your father had. In fact, she was *so* bad she quit right after your father's case ended. She even changed her name and moved away. But I know who she is now, and where she is. And another thing you should know—

Conrad Kramer considers her the love of his life. You could make him hurt the way your dad hurt—the way you and your sister hurt. And of course, I could make it worth your while in the end."

Billy considered the plan. It made sense to him to go after his father's lawyer, who had obviously failed his dad, and who was also someone Conrad Kramer loved. And if it was true there was some kind of financial reward in the end, that was even better. He was tired of struggling all the time.

Genevieve copied down the information Conrad's investigator, Sam, had sent Conrad on the computer on the desk, first for herself, then for Billy. It had given Elizabeth's new name—Kate Roberts—and her current location, some tiny dot on the map in Wisconsin called Farmerton. Genevieve had found the information when she had come early to Conrad's office to meet him for their Valentine's Day lunch date.

When she got to the office a bit earlier than planned, he wasn't there. His laptop was sitting open on his desk. He must have been called away quickly, or just hadn't thought to shut it. She looked at the open laptop, debating her next move. Her curiosity got the better of her and she couldn't help but snoop. In fact, she had been foolish enough to think maybe he was buying her something or making a special plan for the evening. Instead, the page was open to an investigator's report.

As she read it, any hope she had that their marriage could get better flew out the window. Conrad hadn't mentioned Elizabeth for a while now, which had given her hope. She knew they had been engaged on Valentine's Day long ago. He had given her a ring, along with a dozen red roses that night. Conrad never gave Genevieve red roses on Valentine's Day. Instead, she received anything but. She had foolishly let herself believe he may finally have gotten over Elizabeth, but now she knew he was still in love with her, and he had been searching for her all along.

After reading the report, Genevieve had sat down in Conrad's chair and turned around in it to look out the window, thinking about how she was going to call a lawyer after her lunch with Conrad and ask about the steps needed to begin divorce proceedings. That was when Billy had come into the picture. Now, another new plan would be set in motion, too.

After Billy left quietly, Genevieve had moved to a client's chair. With an innocent look on her face, she waited for Conrad to return to his office. He would be surprised to find her there already, but it would be nothing compared to the surprises Genevieve had in store for him.

Chapter 24

The day after Conrad and Genevieve's daughter graduated from high school, Conrad was served divorce papers. He wasn't really all that surprised, to be honest. He knew he was a worthless marital partner, and that his wife deserved better. That's why, even against his lawyer's counsel, he gave Genevieve everything she asked for in her settlement request. She and their daughter should be set for life.

Conrad had moved into the guest room of their large home, then out of the house completely only days after his daughter moved into her dorm room at the University of Chicago. He had purchased a two-bedroom condo, which would be manageable with his reduced income flow. He still had more money and assets than most people and found that he gained little joy from any of it.

In the meantime, Genevieve continued to plan the next steps with Billy and Becky. The divorce had been the first thing on the list for her. Now she, Billy, and Becky had to strategize. She had researched Farmerton and found that its claim to fame was its big Valentine's Day dance.

When Billy and Becky heard about the event on Valentine's Day, they thought it was a sign. Billy mentioned that he had become a very good shot with a deer rifle, having gone with his dad to a quarry shooting tin cans over the years after they no longer hunted. He had access not only to a weapon, but to ammunition as well. Genevieve thought a big event would be best, especially one where no children were present. That way it might look like it was a random shooting and not a targeted murder attempt. It seemed as good a plan as any—until Kate Roberts didn't die.

Had the bullet entered her body a fraction of an inch either way, there would have been a different outcome. Now, Genevieve found herself driving to that forsaken state of Wisconsin for the third time in two weeks. The first time had been to a flower shop that delivered to Farmerton. She had taken Becky with her and had her pay cash for a dozen red roses to be delivered to Kate Roberts at the church where she worked on Valentine's Day. She sent along an envelope with a special little note inside to accompany the order. She had made the one-word message on a friend's computer and printer, telling the friend that hers was being serviced.

The second trip had been to pick up Billy after the shooting. He had driven up in an SUV she had purchased from a man in Kenosha. She had paid cash for it. He signed the title, which she promptly threw into a dumpster at a store. She drove the vehicle to the twins' home and left it there. The plan was that Billy would drive it up to Farmerton with his weapon, flee the scene, then meet Genevieve and his sister at a designated spot from there. Genevieve had even put the meeting spot on the vehicle's GPS, so Billy didn't get confused on those rural roads. He didn't even have a driver's license, but his friend had taught him to drive that fall under the guise that he was going to take his driver's test soon.

Everything seemed to have gone wonderfully, except for one thing. Kate Roberts had survived.

Becky had called the University of Wisconsin Hospital

after the shooting, saying she was a relative. When she found out Kate Roberts was in intensive care, they decided they would have to wait and see what transpired, and if she did indeed survive, they would need yet another plan.

So now Becky and Genevieve sat in Genevieve's vehicle in the outside parking area of the hospital. Genevieve wanted to be able to get out of there as quickly as possible after "it" was done.

Becky had been studying at the community college to become a nurse one day. She had even purchased her first "nurse's scrubs" at a Goodwill Store in anticipation of some clinical work in her next year of study. That all was forgotten after her father's death.

She did remember reading about air embolisms, and that they could cause death, especially when triggered by an IV line. She had been studying harder than she had ever studied while in school over the past week. Genevieve had bought a bag of sodium chloride on the black market, which Becky now had in her large purse. Once she got to the intensive care unit and found out where her "Aunt Kate" was, she would ditch her long coat and purse in the restroom and give Kate Roberts what she deserved.

Billy opened the door, which needed to be replaced, although it was better than their front door. They didn't even use that door anymore and had a sign on it saying to please use the back door. Billy couldn't wait until the day was over. Then they would have their reward. On Monday, he and Becky planned to put their house on the market, then they would split the million dollars in cash and move wherever each of them wanted and do whatever either one of them wanted to do—for once in their lives.

Billy looked at the well-dressed man standing before him. He couldn't believe it. There was Conrad Kramer—right before his eyes. For a moment, he thought Conrad knew what he had done, but he decided to play it cool and see what this man he hated beyond words wanted.

"Yes?" Billy asked, pretending not to know who Conrad was.

"I'm sure you don't remember me, but I knew your father a long time ago. Could I come in for a minute?"

"Okay," Billy found himself saying. Billy stepped back, and Conrad moved into the small kitchen. The room was very outdated, but it was clean and neatly kept. There was a small table against one wall. The appliances and sink were against the others. Behind Billy there appeared to be a grouping of photographs on the wall. Billy shifted his feet, and Conrad could see the large photo of Brian, Billy, and Becky, all smiles, around a dead doe. Then he noticed the rifle above it. He was going to ask about the photo, but first, he had to get down to the business he came to do.

"How did you know my dad?" Billy asked, his arms crossed over his chest. His anger was returning, and his hands balled up into fists.

"I was a lawyer in a case your father was involved in, the one where he was injured. Unfortunately, I made a mistake. I didn't give him a fair deal, so now I'd like to help."

After Conrad said this, he pulled a checkbook out of one pocket, and pen from another.

"You know, my dad lost his job after that case. We had to sell our house and move into this one. Our lives were never the same again, and he died two years ago, after years of financial stress and physical pain that never really went away."

"I'm sorry. I'd like to try to make things right."

"It's too late for that," Billy said angrily. "Nothing you can do can help now." He was seething, and he suddenly and impulsively pulled the loaded rifle down from the wall mount and pointed it at Conrad.

"But this can help make things right, and what my sister is doing to the love of your life up in Madison will help, too." Billy readied the gun.

The shot was deafening. Then all went dark.

Becky found the tower and elevators to the intensive care unit. There was a nurse in scrubs, not unlike the ones she wore under the long coat Genevieve had bought for her to wear. Becky had her hair tied back, like many nurses with longer hair did at work. She started walking down the hall as the real nurse was called away for a moment, saw which room Kate was assigned to on a board, and followed the signs to it. She couldn't wait to see this Elizabeth Kramer/Kate Roberts and get this over with.

Only Kate Roberts wasn't there. Becky went to the nurses' station. Another nurse told her that Kate had been moved to intermediate intensive care and gave her directions to the unit. She even wrote the room number on a piece of paper for her. She mentioned she was so happy that someone from Kate's family had finally surfaced. She told Becky to make sure to leave her contact information with the unit downstairs, or, if she wanted, she could take the information down right then. Becky promised she would give the other unit the information, but she wanted to get going at that moment. She just couldn't wait to see her "aunt."

She followed the simple instructions to the intermediate intensive care unit and surveyed just where the room was located. She decided to change her strategy and found the bathroom. Her heart was pounding as she discarded her coat and put her empty purse in the trash bin. She poked her head out, waiting to make sure there wasn't a nurse at the station near Kate Roberts' room. Then she carried the bag of sodium chloride to the room.

Just as she had hoped, there was no one there except Kate Roberts. Becky walked in and smiled. She asked the woman if she was Kate Roberts, as she knew from her school friend who was doing a practicum that they had to check that it was the right person by having them state their name and birthdate.

Kate Roberts looked different to Becky than she remembered, but she had only been a child. The woman in the bed before her was still attractive, though, even if she was a bit heavier and older. Once she verified that she was indeed Kate, she said she had something for her and showed her the IV bag.

"So, what's this one for?" Kate had asked. She had been poked, prodded, and hooked up to things repeatedly during the past week. She knew all these medicines were making her better, but it was getting tiring.

When the young nurse turned toward the IV, Kate noticed she didn't have a name badge. That seemed strange. She watched as the woman prepared the bag. There was something that seemed familiar about her, but she couldn't place her. She watched the young woman shake the bag and start to lift it. As she did, the nurse finally answered Kate's question.

"It's for my father."

That seemed like a strange answer to Kate's question. But she didn't have much time to think about it as Joe Zimmerman came bursting into the room.

Chapter 25

Not only was there no guard in front of Kate Roberts' room in the ICU, but Pastor Kate wasn't there when Joe poked his head in. That gave him a start. He quickly approached the nurses' station to find out what was going on.

"She's been moved to intermediate care," the nurse told him.

"Is that normal for her to be moved this quickly?"

"Considering she's still fairly young, has general good health, and a strong spirit, it's not inconceivable." The nurse handed him a piece of paper with the new room number. "It's just below us, down one floor. You can use the elevator or the stairs. You can visit her if you want, but you might have to wait. I just gave her niece her room number a minute ago. She was so happy she was out..."

Joe ran off in the middle of the nurse's sentence. To his knowledge, Pastor Kate was not in contact with any of her family members, so whoever went down to see her was most likely not her niece. He thought about how a woman had called the hospital before, wanting information about Kate's condition. His heart pounded, and then his phone rang. Conrad Kramer's name flashed on it, so he put it on speaker as he descended the stairs.

"I'll have to call you back, Mr. Kramer," Joe said, breathing hard as he ran down the staircase.

"Kate's in danger," Conrad said in a weak and breathy voice. "Someone is trying to finish what they started. I can't really talk now, but please, alert someone and have them get to her as soon as possible."

"I'm on my way," Joe said as he stepped onto the floor. He hung up the phone and shouted to the nurse at the station that he was a police officer, and to send security to Kate's room right away.

As he rushed into the room, he saw Kate in the bed, watching a woman dressed in scrubs, who was struggling with the IV. He didn't hesitate. If he was wrong, he was wrong, and he would deal with the consequences of his actions later. He threw his arms around the woman and pinned her to the floor in an arrest hold.

The woman was crying. She turned her head toward Kate and said, "You deserved to die. Why aren't you dead instead of my father?"

Kate didn't know how to answer that, as she didn't know to whom the woman was referring.

Security came rushing to the room, and luckily, they had handcuffs, which Joe used on Becky. He and the security guards watched Becky until a Madison police officer arrived and put her under arrest.

They moved the woman out of Kate's room quickly. Another nurse came in and took Kate's vitals, hoping that this unusual development had not harmed her in any way. She checked the IV equipment to make sure everything was good. The nurse gave a sigh of relief when all checked out. Kate admitted that she had been frightened. She felt good now that she knew Joe was taking care of the situation.

Conrad hated karate classes, but one didn't argue with his mother. Every Saturday morning for five years beginning at age eight, he was dropped off at class. It was the "in" thing for boys at that time. Conrad's mother thought it would give him more confidence, which it probably did, although he would never admit that to her.

He was quite good at it. The instructor had often told him that when he got his black belt, he could be on the competition team. That was the last thing Conrad wanted, so he made certain not to pass his testing. He made it to the green belt, however, despite his best efforts not to advance. One of the younger assistant instructors asked him one day why he didn't want to advance. He could tell Conrad was not demonstrating everything he could do, and would pretend like he didn't know a move when the instructor knew that he could successfully land it.

Conrad simply told the man that it was a long story, and he never asked him again. He didn't want to say that he would do anything to annoy his mother. He had so little power over his life, or her, but in this situation, he had some. Years later, he talked through this passive-aggressive behavior with his therapist.

Well, the day Billy Banyon pointed a gun at him, all those dreaded lessons actually paid off. When he saw the look of hatred in Billy's eyes and heard him click off the safety on his rifle, he sprang into defensive action with a Mae Geri front kick to Billy's chin. It sent him flying backward, but not completely before he got off his shot.

Conrad felt a searing pain in his left shoulder and fell to the floor. Billy fell unconscious to the floor. Conrad was out for a second, but then awakened, looked at Billy, and grabbed the rifle from the floor. He called Joe Zimmerman and told him that he believed Kate to be in imminent danger. Then he dialed 9-1-1.

Conrad propped himself up against a wall and pointed the gun at Billy in case he woke up before the police arrived. Billy was only just starting to stir when they crashed through the door into the kitchen.

After Conrad and Billy were taken to the hospital, Billy was arrested, and both were taken to the precinct for questioning. Conrad told the authorities everything he knew, and why he had gone to Billy's that day. Billy wasn't saying much, especially about his sister, but he did bring up a name in his interview with the police.

Billy had implicated Conrad's ex-wife, Genevieve, as being involved in the case. Apparently, she had promised the twins a million dollars when their "mission" had been completed.

At the jail in the City-County Building in Madison, Becky Banyon would not implicate her brother, but she had no qualms about mentioning Genevieve Markwell Kramer. She told the officers that Genevieve had been planning to pay them a million dollars to accomplish this "mission." Genevieve had told them it was a win-win situation for both her and them.

When the detective asked her how they might contact Ms. Kramer, Becky answered, "She was waiting for me in the parking lot at the hospital."

After giving the officers a description of Genevieve and her car, a black Mercedes-Benz sedan with Illinois license plates, they took Becky back to holding. Joe went with one of the officers back to the hospital. They decided not to use their lights and sirens. If Genevieve was still there, they would have a better chance if they could sneak up on her.

Genevieve was starting to become concerned. It was closing in on an hour, and still no Becky. She knew that it was a huge hospital, and it took some time to get around. She also knew that sometimes patients were out of their rooms, having tests or other procedures done, and that this could affect the amount of time Becky needed to complete her assignment.

Every time Genevieve heard a siren—which was often at a large hospital—she jumped a little. She checked her phone and saw that she had a text from her daughter. Marissa wanted to know if they could have lunch together the following Friday, a day when she only had one early morning class. Marissa wanted to discuss an internship she had been offered for the summer. They planned to meet at one of their favorite restaurants, not far from campus. Genevieve loved her daughter. At least Conrad had given her one good thing over the years.

She hit send, then heard a little knock on the car window. She thought it was Becky and that the car door must have been locked. But when she looked up, there was a man in a blue uniform at her window. Then she noticed a female officer in front of her, another officer behind her, and a man in plainclothes standing at the passenger window. She knew it was no use trying to flee and put up her hands in surrender.

Once at the jail, Genevieve tried to convince the officers that she had no choice in the matter at hand—that she had been held at knifepoint by Billy and had acquiesced to his plan to kill Kate Roberts. She failed to mention that it had been a year ago when they initially met, that Billy had wanted to kill Conrad, not Kate, and that she had many opportunities to report the incident since that time.

The detective then spoke to Becky, who filled him in on the timeline of the plan and how it had begun a year ago. Just then, an officer came in and told the detective they had found a suitcase in the trunk of Genevieve's car containing a million dollars in cash, just like Becky had told them. Genevieve made a phone call to her lawyer, then was taken to a cell.

Becky asked if someone could call her brother and tell him what had happened to her. They did, but found out that he was also in jail and could not receive any phone calls. He was under arrest for the attempted murder of Conrad Kramer.

Chapter 26

Conrad was in utter disbelief when he received the call from Genevieve's lawyer telling him what had happened and that he should inform any interested parties in the family. Conrad's first thought, and his priority, was his daughter. For a man who usually knew exactly what to say in every situation, this was completely new territory for him. He struggled as he broke the news to his sweet girl and heard her sobbing on the other end of the phone. He offered to come and get her, but she said not to—not yet anyway. Maybe the next weekend. Conrad felt it was better than a flat-out "no."

Conrad knew this process could be long and difficult. He had agreed to post Genevieve's bail, if she was given that option and if Genevieve's parents somehow couldn't come up with enough money. He only agreed to that because his daughter had begged him. Fortunately, he never had to do that, as her family had enough resources, and, after more information had been uncovered, Genevieve was not granted bail. At least his daughter knew he would have been willing to help had the occasion arisen.

Conrad's shoulder was aching badly. He took some over-the-counter medication, sat in the recliner he rarely used, and put his feet up. The last thing he needed right now was any complication to his injury. He knew he was supposed to get a lot of rest, which was not in his wheelhouse. Surprisingly, for a man who never napped and slept only six hours every night, Conrad fell asleep, exhausted from the stressful and unusual events of the day.

Joe got into his SUV and began his drive back to Farmerton. He was much later than he had planned, and he called Jodie.

"Joe! I was getting worried about you. I sent you a couple of texts and didn't hear back from you."

"I'm so sorry, sweetheart. But I'm on my way home now. You won't believe what happened today."

"Is Pastor Kate all right?"

"She is, but she almost wasn't."

Joe filled Jodie in on all the details of the day's events. Jodie had heard many crazy stories over the past eight years in law enforcement, but this one sounded like something right out of Hollywood.

"I'm so glad you were there in time, Joe. You saved her life."

Joe thought about that for a second. He guessed Jodie was right.

"I suppose I did," he said, and smiled. He felt like he had paid Pastor Kate back just a little bit for all the help she had given Jodie and him over the past two years.

An hour later, he pulled into his driveway, happy to be back in this quiet little town, and relieved to be ahead of the snowstorm, which was supposed to come their way that evening. He had stopped for milk and bread at the convenience store on the edge of town—he, and everyone else in Farmerton. Now, he was ready to hug his wife and maybe get that blasted crib put together.

Once he got inside the house, though, Joe felt like he had been hit by a bomb. All the adrenaline from earlier in the day wore away. He fell into his favorite, well-loved chair and was fast asleep in moments. He didn't wake up until Jodie told him it was time for dinner.

They talked all through dinner about their theories as to why this had all happened. They only had the bits and pieces of the story at this point—the information Becky, Billy, and Genevieve had shared, any of which may or may not have been true.

Then they talked about Conrad going over to Billy's house.

"I had called him to tell him that Pastor Kate was all right and asked him how he had known about her being in danger. He said he had gone to the twins' home to apologize for the rotten deal he had convinced their father to take, and to give them the money their father should have received long ago. He wanted to help make things right. Billy had told him it was too late for that, but that his sister was going to take care of that up in Madison. Apparently, that was when Billy became irate. He pulled a mounted rifle from the wall and pointed it at Conrad.

"When Conrad heard a click, he gave Billy a karate kick. Billy fell back from the kick at the same time he got a shot off. The bullet hit Conrad's shoulder but exited. He should be fine. Ballistics has the gun now and are almost positive it's the same weapon used to shoot Pastor Kate. Pastor Kate is one lucky person. Not everyone survives two attempts on their life."

"Lucky, or, as she would probably say, blessed," Jodie commented.

"You're right on that."

After dinner, the couple decided to watch a movie, just to get their minds off reality for a while. Joe knew he should be working on that crib, but he just didn't have the energy.

After the movie ended, Jodie headed to bed. She had fallen asleep and missed the ending of the show. She would have to catch it another time. She was just so tired all the time these days.

Joe decided to stay up for a while. He wrote up the day's incidents on his computer. He had not been on duty, technically, but had most likely done some of the most important work in his career on this day. He was just happy to have gotten there in time. He also felt happy in some way for Conrad Kramer. It seemed to Joe that the man might truly have a heart. And then Joe thought—a heart that still belonged to Pastor Kate.

Joe checked the outside temperature using his cell phone. It was thirty-seven degrees and dropping, and the wind was making it feel colder. Ideal conditions for every cop's nightmare—ice. Just then his phone alerted him to an ice storm approaching at a rapid pace, and a communication from the Sheriff's Department that said road closures were expected overnight.

Joe heard rain pelting against the window and was so glad it was the weekend. Of course, this probably meant there would be no auction the next afternoon, and wondered how they would end up handling the situation. Joe felt so thankful that he was currently off shift. Little did he know, however, that he would shortly be called into duty in a new and unexpected way.

◆

Joe easily drifted off to sleep. It had been a day—no, make that a week. He had been sleeping soundly when he was awakened by an unfamiliar sound. At first, he thought he was just dreaming, and shut his eyes again. He had almost fallen back asleep when he heard it again. His cell phone said it was just past two a.m. He turned to see if Jodie was awake and had heard the sound, too, but she wasn't in bed. He assumed she was making one of her usual nighttime runs to the bathroom, but when she didn't emerge after a few minutes, he became concerned.

He waited another minute, then sat up and dragged himself out of bed. His legs felt like lead as he trudged to the bathroom. He stopped and listened, then gently knocked on the door.

"Everything okay in there, Jodie?"

A moment later, she opened the door, a strange look on her face.

"I'm not sure, Joe, but something is going onnnn—" She stopped and wrapped her arms around herself, grimacing. When the tightness in her midsection subsided, she pulled her cell out of her pocket and looked at the time.

"Since I've never gone through this before, I can't be sure, but I think I might be having some sort of contractions. It's probably just Braxton Hicks. The doctor told me those false labor contractions sometimes occur in late pregnancy. I'm going to take a warm bath and drink some water—two things she said might be helpful."

Joe was trying, quite unsuccessfully, not to panic. He looked at his own phone, which indicated the storm had arrived and he could hear the icy rain still hitting the roof and windows.

"Can I do anything to help?" Joe asked, feeling utterly useless.

"Not yet, and hopefully not at all. Go back to sleep," Jodie said, trying to sound confident.

Joe knew getting back to sleep was completely out of the question. He walked down the hall to the dining room and looked out of the sliding glass door, turning on the deck light. The deck glistened with a thick coat of ice.

Just then, his phone dinged with news that the highways in the area were now closed to traffic until further notice, and he felt sick to his stomach. What if these contractions were the real thing? What then? He tried to remember his training, but it felt like a thousand years ago. Even the things they had learned in their recent childbirth classes seemed hazy. Joe knew he had to pull himself together, though. He would be worthless if he didn't.

He thought about what he could do. Just in case, he gathered some towels and blankets from a large linen closet in the hallway and put them on the chair in the nursery. He looked around at the changing table they had put up, and some of the items on it they had received as a part of a shower in their honor. There was a syringe bulb, baby wipes, ointment, and newborn diapers in a compartment on the table. In the closet were the tiniest clothes he had ever seen hanging on small plastic hangers. Ridiculously soft baby blankets with satin bindings were at the ready on a shelf, along with thinner swaddling blankets. Everything was good, except for that crib still leaning against the wall.

After Joe gathered his emergency items, he turned off the light in the room. He checked to make certain his phone was fully charged, which it was. He knew he was most likely overreacting, but he wanted to be prepared. As his late grandmother used to say, "rather safe than sorry." He smiled as he thought about his grandma, and wished she was still around so she could meet their baby—and the baby could meet her. She had always been Joe's go-to person, especially after his dad died and his mother followed his sister and her family to another community. But even before that, they had shared a special bond.

Joe hurried back to the bedroom and sat on the bed. A small lamp on its lowest setting filled the room with a soft glow. He watched the bathroom door and looked expectantly at Jodie as she emerged in a soft terry robe, the bottom fringes of her hair damp. She slipped into bed and asked him to hold her.

"You're feeling better, I take it?" Joe asked.

"I will be if you hold me," she said.

"That I can do," he said, and put his arm around her, snuggling up to her back and feeling a slight sense of relief. Jodie quickly fell asleep, and Joe shortly followed. But their rest was short-lived.

An hour later, Jodie had another contraction. This was stronger and longer than the ones she had experienced earlier. Joe recorded the time in his phone. Another one came in five minutes, and then another after another five minutes. He knew that wasn't good.

Jodie said she had to use the restroom again and walked to the bathroom, just as her water broke. After that, the contractions came every three minutes. Joe gathered all the towels and blankets from the nursery and brought them back into the bedroom. They made a makeshift hospital bed, using an old mattress pad out of the linen closet between some old sheets to protect the bed.

Joe called the dispatcher, who said they would try to get someone to them as soon as they could, but right now, one couldn't even stand up on the ground, and any vehicles that had been on the road earlier were now in ditches, some with their occupants still inside. Plows were trying to get salt down, but the rain kept coming, making it difficult to improve the road conditions. Two plows had recently slid off the road as well. At this point, it was almost more hazardous to have them on the road than not.

Joe called their doctor, but the call went to voicemail, which gave the number of a physician who was on-call for their regular doctor. He could try the other number, but things were happening so quickly. Joe felt like he was having a bad dream, except he wasn't. If not for his calm wife, he may have completely lost it. She helped him stay on track, even though the pains were getting more and more intense and almost constant at this point. So, with Jodie's encouragement, Joe was beginning to think he could do this, and then they heard a crack and the lights went out.

Joe took out his cell phone and walked carefully to the window. He looked out and saw only darkness. The power outage was affecting his entire neighborhood, and most likely all of Farmerton. He called the power company just in case no one else had. He knew they would not be able to start working on it until the weather changed and roads opened.

He went to the garage using his phone flashlight and took the emergency kit he had in the trunk to the bedroom. He had a high-powered emergency light that should last at least eight hours. The light could help him see better, but it would do nothing to help the other issue at hand. It was only in the thirties outside, and the temperature in the house was going to begin falling quickly. Not exactly a welcoming environment for an early baby.

He texted Simon about the situation, even though it was doubtful his friend would see the text until the morning. Simon wouldn't be able to do anything to help him, even if he saw it, but it made Joe feel better, nonetheless. He needed to tell someone what was going on.

Jodie had lit a vanilla-scented candle she kept on the nightstand, then climbed back into the bed as Joe entered the room. He was just going to ask her how she was feeling when she answered his question by groaning and gritting her teeth.

Joe sat down on the bed next to her and held her hand. She looked pretty in the candlelight, even when wincing in pain. The contractions were coming even more quickly now, and Jodie scooted into position, knowing it would soon be time to push.

Joe moved as well, hoping and praying that he could hold himself together for the sake of his wife and soon-appearing child. He positioned his light and was surprised to see the top of the baby's head. He told Jodie that on her next contraction, she should start to push.

"Gladly," she said, drawing a deep breath and gearing up for the birth event. He was sorry he couldn't hold her, but it was more important for him to be delivering than coaching.

On the next contraction, Jodie pushed. She pushed on the next, and on the next, the baby's entire head and neck were out. Joe was not prepared for what he saw, though. The umbilical cord was wrapped around the baby's neck. He tried not to panic and show it on his face, but Jodie noticed the look right away.

"What's wrong?" she asked.

"Ah, the baby's just a little tangled up. As soon as it's out a bit more..." He didn't get to say anything else as Jodie gave a huge grunt and pushed as hard as she could. To his amazement, the body was almost completely out. He gently took the cord and unwrapped it from the baby's neck, hoping the child was okay. He knew babies were not always the most responsive at birth, so he would just have to wait and see when the child was out, which happened in a matter of seconds.

Joe looked down in amazement and began rubbing the baby's body with his large, warm hands. Finally, the child began to cry. Tears of joy ran down his cheeks as he quickly wiped the tiny body with a soft baby washcloth, then wrapped him in a soft, thick towel and laid him on Jodie's chest. "Here's your son," he said to her softly.

"It's a boy?" She looked at Joe, tearing up. She just gazed at the tiny human on her chest. "Hello, Jake Joseph," she said lovingly, stroking the side of the baby's cheek.

Joe became very emotional upon hearing the name she had chosen. There had never been a doubt about the baby's first name if it were a boy. Jake had been Jodie's late brother's name. But the middle name they had deliberated unsuccessfully until Joe told her a couple of weeks before that she should pick the middle name, as she was the one carrying the load in this pregnancy—literally. Since then, Jodie had been hush-hush about her middle name choice.

Joe delivered the placenta, removed the dirty towels and folded sheet from underneath his wife, and put some new ones down. As foolish as he had once thought it was to have all those extra towels and sheets that took up an entire closet, he was now very happy to have them. Then he turned his attention back to his wife and child.

"How do you feel, Jodie?" Joe asked, then touched the baby's soft head. The baby turned his face toward Joe just a bit and Joe was stunned by the response. This was a real human being—someone who felt his touch, someone Joe knew immediately that he would love to the day he died.

Jodie smiled at him. "I'm in love," she responded.

Joe smiled at her, knowing exactly what she felt, and answered, "Me, too."

"Jake Joseph is even more handsome than his daddy," Jodie mentioned.

"That wouldn't take much," Joe said in his usual self-deprecating manner. "But he is a handsome little guy, isn't he?"

Joe kissed Jodie softly, then the baby's head. He went to the nursery, where he had seen a little hat someone had knitted. He brought it back and put it on the baby's head to help keep him warm. Then they just stared at their child for a few minutes.

Jodie pulled the comforter up to cover them both as reality started to set in once more. It was getting colder in the room, and she didn't want the newborn to catch a chill. It was startling enough for a baby to be outside of the warm waters of the womb, let alone to be in a room where the temperature was falling. At least it wasn't a sub-zero night.

But Joe was concerned. How long could he keep them both warm? Was the baby truly okay, considering he had had a cord wrapped around his neck for who knows how long? It was 3:30 a.m. on February twenty-third. Joe wrote the time and date of birth into his phone, although it was doubtful he would ever forget any part of this event for as long as he lived.

Joe used his cellphone flashlight to go downstairs and start a fire in the lower-level fireplace. They had two fireplaces in the house; one he could easily switch on—provided there was power available—the other in the basement rec room, which was wood-fired. It had been a compromise—Jodie liked the simplicity and cleaner version on the main level, while he liked the good old-fashioned wood-burning version. He loved the smell of it, especially when he was watching a Packers game on a cold Sunday afternoon.

Joe left the door to the basement open to the upstairs, hoping some of the heat would rise, but he knew it wouldn't be enough. He sincerely hoped he wouldn't have to move his family downstairs. It didn't sound like a good or safe option. He would do it only if the situation became dire. His family. He had to let that word settle in. He was a father. Jodie was a mother. They had a son. They were a family. He returned to the bedroom, eyes stinging with tears.

Half an hour passed. Joe had cut the umbilical cord as instructed by their doctor, who they had finally reached, despite her being out of town and not on call. They didn't want to talk to a stranger. She didn't mind at all, considering the situation, but she wished that she could be of more help. She gave them some ideas of what they should do, but also mentioned that as soon as the roads were open, Jodie and the baby should be transported to St. Mary's Hospital in Madison. She was going to call and make sure everyone was prepared to carry out this plan, but they all knew it could still be hours until this was feasible.

It was starting to feel cold in the room. They could hear the ice-covered branches outside tinkling like wind chimes as they slapped together in the wind. The sound was making Joe very nervous, but then he heard another sound. It sounded like a motor of some sort. He looked out the window but couldn't see anything.

There was a knock on the front door, which made both him and Jodie jump. Who could possibly be out in this weather?

Joe made his way to the front door and opened it slowly. There stood Jack, one of Simon's employees, who had done work previously on their home remodeling project.

"Simon said you have a baby coming?" Jack stood with ice cleats strapped to his boots. A portable generator and electric heater sat at his feet as he stood under the covered overhang of the house. He had made his way to the house driving his special ice fishing all-terrain vehicle, which was able to maneuver on ice—in fact, that was what it was made for.

"He's here already," Joe announced.

"Take these. Let's hook up the cord right here," Jack said, pointing to an outdoor outlet. "Then you can hook up the heater and anything else you want to hook up to the generator with this." Jack showed Joe an extremely long, heavy-duty electrical cord with multiple outlets at its end. "This should hold you until they can get the power back on."

"Jack—I don't know how to thank you," Joe said, getting choked up.

"No worries," Jack responded, a man of few words. He was a man of action.

Jack turned on the generator and helped hook up the cord. They kept the generator on the small porch, closing the front door as far as they could with the cord in it.

Joe carried the heater and main cord with its outlets and maneuvered his way back to the bedroom, his cell phone lighting the way. Joe would hook one small lamp up when he got to the room, along with the heater. He vowed to himself that he would be purchasing a home generator as soon as possible. He never wanted to be in a situation like this again with a baby in the house.

Joe hooked up the lamp next to the bed, then quickly got the heater going, which was amazingly effective. He got an extension cord and hooked up the refrigerator. Those were the most important things to keep going until the power returned.

Joe, now feeling calmer, took a photo of Jodie holding Jake. Then he took a turn posing for the camera with Jake. He couldn't believe how little he was, and held him like he was a piece of chinaware. Afterward, Joe opened his shirt and put the baby against his chest as they had been taught in childbirth classes. It was a feeling he had never experienced before. This tiny, warm body against his. This little one was a part of him, and a part of Jodie, yet was his own little being.

Joe had gotten some little kind of little "bed" that looked like a dog bed to him out of the nursery closet. Jodie told him to put it on the bed next to her. Once it was toasty warm in the room, she laid Jake on his back in the center of it. She had wrapped him like an expert into a tight little cocoon in one of the thin blankets.

"There, he should be good for a bit—until he gets hungry, which won't be long," she said, smiling. "But for a moment, let's try to get some rest."

Joe wasn't about to argue with her. He was wiped out. Joe decided he would have to write down everything that happened during the week leading up to Jake's birth so he could read it to him someday. Otherwise, Jake would probably think his dad was making it up. Joe sat in the armchair, while Jodie and Jake shared the bed. He smiled at the scene, then fell asleep.

Little Jake made it almost an hour and a half before he needed to be fed. Jodie was nervous about breastfeeding for the first time, but the little guy didn't seem to be complaining. She was glad she had bought some formula, too, just in case it was needed.

At half-past six in the morning, dawn began to break in Farmerton. The wind had died down an hour before and the temperature had been rising rapidly. By seven, the sun was shining on the icy wonderland outside. Joe noticed that the forecast was for a high of forty-eight degrees by early that afternoon. That was Wisconsin weather, for certain.

He poured himself a bowl of cereal, then made a small tray with a bowl for Jodie along with a small glass of orange juice. He was happy to have a bit of natural light to guide his way. Just as he was carrying her breakfast down to her, the lights and heat snapped back on. Joe heard Jodie exclaim "Hallelujah" from the bedroom and said one of his own. Then the baby began to cry, making his presence known.

After Joe delivered the breakfast—which, of course, Jodie wouldn't get to eat immediately because Jake wanted to be fed—he texted Simon to see if he was up yet. He was awake, so Joe called him.

"Simon," Joe said. "I have a son." He was getting emotional again.

"I hope our children will be good friends, like you and me."

"Me too," answered Joe. "And thank you so much for sending Jack to my place. Because of his and your kindness, Jodie and the baby were able to stay warm."

"How is the little one?"

"Well, as far as we know, good, but soon a medical transport will arrive and take both Jodie and the baby to St. Mary's in Madison. Both need to be checked out thoroughly."

"That makes sense, especially with him coming a little early."

Joe smiled. "I guess Jake Joseph was as anxious to meet us as we were to meet him. I'll have to be careful what I say in the future, as I had just remarked yesterday that I couldn't wait to meet our child."

"I understand the feeling," Simon said. Joe could almost hear his smile.

Just then there was a knock on the door. Joe saw that it was Jodie and Jake's ride to Madison.

"I've got to go now, Simon. But thanks again, for everything. If you ever need anything, I'm here for you."

"I know you are. Now, get going!"

Joe followed the vehicle all the way to the hospital in Madison. Before he left, he texted the photos of the baby to Pastor Kate and told her she had to get better soon so she could baptize Jake Joseph Zimmerman. She texted back that this was an amazing surprise. She congratulated the couple, telling Joe he had made her day, and that she felt better just looking at those precious photos.

Chapter 27

On Monday, everything seemed to be calming down. The weather was in the low fifties, and the organizers of the twice-postponed Valentine's Day auction sent emails, made phone calls, and even put out a radio advertisement that they would have the auction that evening. There were no school events scheduled, miraculously, and the women of the churches did not want their pies and punch ingredients to go to waste.

Even though there would be no orchestra, the event ended up with record-breaking bids in the end. People in Farmerton were in great spirits and felt very generous, especially upon hearing that arrests had been made in the shooting case. It made everyone feel safer. They felt relieved to be able to put another painful piece of Farmerton history to rest.

Even Sissy attended the auction. She was tired by the end of the evening, but she was so happy to get out of the house. She would be returning to work the next day, which made her customers and colleagues very happy. She enjoyed a piece of pie that evening, declaring it the best she had ever tasted. Sissy did skip the ice cream, however, trying to follow her stricter diet to some extent. Her husband, Jon, a notoriously frugal man, made the largest bid of the entire auction in her honor. He had been saving money for a fishing boat but used it on the bid instead. Sissy declared it to be the most romantic thing he had ever done in their thirty years of marriage. She was also grateful for Jon contacting his accountant friend, who had come up with a brilliant plan to help her repay her debt and keep her shop. Sissy was one very happy and relieved woman.

Joe had talked to reporters in Madison in between holding his newborn and his wife. He was also sent on an errand by Jodie to buy a bassinet for their room at home. The baby would sleep in it in their room with them until he got a little bigger. That would also give Joe some more time to get that blasted crib set up.

Jake was given a clean bill of health and was transferred to the regular care nursery. Jodie was doing well, too, and they would both go home the next day. Jodie was a little dehydrated, but an intravenous drip, along with lots of water and juice, was quickly taking care of that issue. She met with the lactation expert and then both she and Joe got lessons on baths and other newborn care tips. Once again, Joe felt overwhelmed, but he had never been so happy in his life.

Conrad did a rare thing on Monday. He took the day off. His nephew and sister covered his agenda for the day, which was light by his standards. He had said he was going to rest, but what he really planned to do was visit Genevieve, whose custody had now been transferred to their area.

He wasn't sure exactly why he wanted to see her. Perhaps it was for their daughter's sake.

It was even stranger than he had imagined seeing her in a jumpsuit from the jail, rather than the designer clothes she usually wore.

Her hair was pulled back into a ponytail, which he wasn't sure he had ever seen before in all their years together.

She sat at the cold steel table. He took a seat across from her. Conrad wasn't sure how to begin the conversation, but he didn't have to.

"What do you want, Conrad?" Genevieve asked in an angry tone.

"I just wanted to see how you were doing."

"How does it look like I'm doing?" she retorted.

They were both quiet for a minute.

"Is there anything I can do—"

She cut him off. "You've done quite enough, Conrad."

"I'm sorry, Genevieve. I do care about you. You're the mother of my child."

"Save it," she said coolly.

"How could you hate me so much, Genevieve?"

"You made it incredibly easy."

Conrad felt a slight sting, but she was probably correct. He wasn't sure how much more there was to say, especially considering Genevieve's current state of mind. He did have one more question for her, however.

"Did you really think you would get away with this?"

"I've been watching you get people out of worse situations than this for years, so I didn't worry about it too much."

That one made him wince. "Again, I'm sorry," he said, rising from his seat.

"Yes, you *are*."

Conrad didn't see any point in continuing this conversation any longer. He walked to the door and knocked on it for the officer to let him out.

Jodie needed to get some rest in between Jake's feedings. She suggested Joe visit Pastor Kate since she was only a few miles away, and Joe, tired of sitting in the uncomfortable hospital furniture in their room, was eager to move. He asked if there was anything he could bring her on the way back. She really wanted a glass of wine, but that would have to wait until the next night when they were home.

Joe was eager to visit the pastor, as he didn't really get to visit her the day before due to the fiasco that had taken place. This time they could truly talk to each other, and, of course, Joe arrived armed with a new arsenal of photos to show her.

Kate was sitting up reading when he arrived. She was surprised to see him, but very happy to have a chance to thank him in person for his rescue of her the day before.

"You're a real lifesaver, Joe. In many ways. I can't thank you enough," she said.

"Well, I'm just glad my timing worked out. When I got a call telling me you might be in grave danger, I just hoped I wasn't too late."

"You got a call? From whom?"

"Ah, are you certain you want to know?"

"Is there a reason I wouldn't? Please, tell me who else I should thank."

"You'll probably be surprised by this, but it was Conrad."

Kate looked blankly for a moment. "Conrad—as in Conrad Kramer?"

"One and the same."

Joe went on to tell her all about the plan that had been

hatched over a year's time from one Valentine's Day to the next. When she had survived the shooting, a new plan had to be improvised, which led to Becky coming to Madison to finish the "mission," as they had put it.

Then Joe told her the other events that had transpired on Saturday—how Conrad had gone to the Banyon house, wanting to make amends, having no idea that Billy had been involved in her shooting, and that he had almost been killed.

Pastor Kate looked at Joe incredulously.

"We are talking about the man to whom I used to be married, correct?"

"Yes. From the little interaction I've had with him, and his actions the other day, I think he might be a different person than when you knew him."

"I hope so," she said quietly. "I guess we all can change over time, can't we?"

Joe nodded and, echoing the pastor's words, said, "I hope so." He was thinking back to his own younger days, when his first marriage dissolved badly and he had "let himself go," physically and mentally. Joe was no longer that person, thankfully. And now he was a new dad.

"Speaking of changes, I've got some more photos of Jake to bore you with."

"I could never get bored looking at photos of that sweet little baby." Kate took his phone and scrolled through the many photos. She particularly enjoyed a photo of all three of them together that a nurse had taken, and one of Jake yawning. She suddenly felt a bit sad that she had never had the chance to be a mother.

"Can I send myself some of these photos?" she asked.

"Of course."

Kate forwarded her favorites and handed the phone back to a smiling Joe. It was fun to see him so proud and excited. Kate knew how hard he worked, and Jodie, too, and that it was work very few people wanted to or could do. The couple deserved some happiness, and she was grateful to see it unfold.

Joe stood up, saying he should probably get back to the other hospital. Then he would go home until the next morning. This afternoon, he would put up the new bassinet he had bought after he got home. It would take only a matter of minutes. He also had to get the new infant car seat into the back of his vehicle for the ride home the next day.

Joe thought Jodie and Jake would be released around noon. Jodie's parents were coming at nine o'clock to meet Jake, and he planned to be there when they arrived. They were so excited and had been very touched by Jake's namesake.

Joe squeezed the pastor's hand and was on his way, smiling from ear to ear, then left the room and the hospital. It was a completely different experience than it had been the day before. One of the nurses called out to him as he left, "Have a good day, superhero!"

After Joe left, Pastor Kate stared out the window. It was a pretty winter day, but she really didn't notice the weather or scenery. She just couldn't get over Conrad going to the Banyon house to apologize and offer them money. And she especially couldn't believe he had helped save her life. She had some thinking to do—or, more accurately, some praying.

Joe had so much good adrenaline in his system when he

returned home that not only did he get the car seat in and set up the bassinet, but he even got the crib put together. After the last screw was tightened and the mattress settled inside, Joe stood back and admired it. He thought it looked classy—for a baby bed.

Joe finally sat down, had a sandwich, and watched some college hoops on television. It was between two teams he really didn't care about, which was perfect. After half an hour of this mindless activity, he turned off the television, carried his plate to the kitchen, and put it in the dishwasher, then went down the hall toward the bedroom. He texted Jodie a photo of the bassinet and crib, then climbed into his own bed. He looked at photos from earlier in the day once again. He turned off the light, said a little prayer of thanks, and promptly fell asleep.

Kate finished her hospital meal of meatloaf and mashed potatoes, thankful that the food tasted better than it had looked. Then she looked at her phone sitting on the tray table. She tried to watch television, but her eyes kept gravitating back to her phone. She wanted to call Conrad. *What was she thinking?* She had just spent the better part of the past twenty years trying to escape him, putting him out of her mind and making it as hard as she could for him to find out who she had become or where she was. But her heart won out over her mind this time.

She was unsure if she should make the call, but she realized how much she *wanted* to. She picked up the phone and punched in the number she still had memorized.

"Hello, Conrad?" Kate said into the phone.

A voice answered, "Yes."

"This is..." She hesitated, not knowing which name she should give.

"I know who you are—Kate." He spoke her name in such a gentle tone that she barely recognized his voice.

Kate could hardly breathe, and her heart was racing. She feared she was going to set off alarms on the machine she was still hooked up to for at least one more day. The doctor had told her that she might be able to move into a regular room if she kept making the kind of progress she was currently achieving. Right now, she wasn't certain she would live another day the way her heart was pounding against her chest.

"I probably shouldn't be bothering you, but I just wanted to say thank you. Joe Zimmerman told me you called him to warn him I was in danger. He also told me the other things you had done, at the Banyon house."

"It probably wasn't my wisest move. I should have known offering an apology and money way too many years late could never come close to easing the pain they had suffered. And I certainly underestimated the response I could receive," Conrad said.

"How is your injury?" Kate asked, finding herself genuinely caring about his welfare.

"I'm doing well. But the bigger question is, how are *you* doing?" he asked.

Kate was struck by the fact that Conrad had deflected attention away from himself and asked about her. This was something new.

"They may move me to a regular room in two or three days. And if things go well, I may get to go home by the end of next week. I'll have to do some physical therapy—they already started a little yesterday, but I can live—*literally*—with that."

Conrad laughed lightly. Kate could almost see his dimples and the way the lines crinkled around his cornflower-blue eyes.

"That is truly wonderful news," he said.

Kate wasn't sure what to say next. She couldn't tell him that the thought had crossed her mind at one point that he had shot her, even though she had never known him to use a gun.

"Kate," he said again, tenderly. "I need to make a confession—confessions. The reason my ex-wife and the Banyons found out where you were was because I left a report my investigator had sent me about you open on my laptop in my office, and Genevieve saw it. I am so sorry."

Conrad continued, "I was so excited when I learned about you. It was the hardest thing I've ever done not contacting you." He hesitated. "But here's my other confession. Two weeks ago on a Saturday, thinking about Valentine's Day coming up—well—I weakened. I drove to your home. I caught a glimpse of you through a window. A dog started barking in your neighborhood and I ran off, knocking over your garbage can. Again, I'm sorry. But, worst of all, I noticed your scarf on the ground by your mailbox."

He hesitated again. "I took it. I am sorry. I know your mother made it, and I will get it back to you as soon as possible. I can send it to your church. Again, I am so sorry. I disappointed myself, and my therapist, and, of course, you—once again. I confessed this to my therapist a couple days ago. She agreed it wasn't a good move on my part, but she tells me she will forgive me. I hope you might, too, one day." His voice sounded very sad and sincere as he relayed this information.

Kate was quiet for a minute. She was thinking. It was a lot to process. But more than anything that he had told her, she was stunned by his honesty and his apologies. She couldn't think of a time when Conrad Kramer had ever said he was sorry—for anything.

"Kate, are you there?"

"Yes, I am. You don't need to send the scarf. I have a better idea."

Chapter 28

On Easter Sunday, Jake was baptized at St. John's Church. Joe and Jodie, along with Jake's sponsors, Simon and Sally, stood around the font as Pastor Kate did the honors. It was a great day, although Joe and Jodie were sad that the very next Sunday would be Pastor Kate's last Sunday serving at the church. The church was planning a luncheon after the service in her honor, as many people loved her and would miss her.

Pastor Kate had decided it was time for her to move on. Her work in Farmerton was done. She would begin a new call in the fall, this time a permanent position in a small congregation just outside of Madison, whose pastor was retiring. It would be her first assignment in a congregation that was not in crisis, and she was looking forward to it, although she knew that anything could happen in any congregation—one could just ask the members of St. John's in

Farmerton about that.

She had just signed a year's lease on a beautiful two-bedroom apartment in Madison, a town she dubbed as the perfect blend of city and small town. She bought a bike and looked forward to using it on the extensive trail system in the area.

But, most importantly, during her time off from work in the summer months, Kate planned to do a different type of "work" of her own. She would begin with a visit to her parents and brother in Iowa. It was time to practice what she preached about forgiveness and how people could become new creations and start over.

She already had begun her personal assignment by meeting with Conrad. She and Conrad had gotten together at a coffee shop in Madison a few weeks after she had first called him, when she was out of the hospital and well enough to be out and about. She had told him on the phone that day in the hospital that he could return her scarf to her in person, which he did.

They had ended up talking for hours. She was still amazed by his change in behavior and attitude. He had even asked her what she would like when he ordered for them at the counter, instead of assuming he knew what she would want, as he had always done in the past. He had mentioned during their discussion that he was finally starting to feel like the person he was meant to be—the best version of himself.

Kate was so impressed by his obvious gains in therapy that she decided to sign on for the services of the counselor she had referred Jodie to after her abduction. Kate was currently feeling happier and enjoying a sense of freedom she hadn't felt in many years. As for what might come of her relationship with Conrad, she figured only time would tell.

On August fifth, Jacklyn Jo came into the world into the arms and hearts of her parents, Simon and Sally. They named their daughter after their favorite people—Jack, Joe, and Jodie. She was a sweet and pretty dark-haired baby who loved to be held, and her parents were happy to oblige.

Joe, Jodie, and Jake came to meet her when she got home from the hospital. Jake was a very active baby now. He rolled all over the place, was sitting up on his own, and was just about ready to crawl. He was a good sleeper, though, which helped his parents tremendously.

Jodie had decided to stay working administratively after her parental leave ended, at least for a while. She did miss being out in the field but had decided that one parent putting their life in danger every day on the job was enough for one family.

Joe was back helping with the Farmerton High School football team as one of its assistant coaches. He particularly worked with the quarterbacks, the position he had starred in as a player at the very same school. The boys on the team had given him a little Farmerton Falcons sweatshirt for Jake, which should fit him perfectly by the time the season started. Joe was very touched by their thoughtfulness.

Joe was also working with the school administration on some new safety equipment and measures for the school. It had been far too easy for a shooter to enter the Valentine's Day Dance. It would be even more tragic if something like that happened during a school event. He was going to do everything in his power to keep that from occurring.

On Valentine's Day the next year, Kate met Conrad for dinner out in Milwaukee, her traveling from Madison, him from Chicago. They went to a restaurant Kate had heard about when the chef had been a participant on a television cooking show. Conrad had greeted her with a sweet smile and a single pink rose. He said that pink was supposed to be the color of health. They sat down and looked at the menu, and then Conrad asked Kate what she recommended they order.

Farmerton had once again held its Valentine's fundraiser event. Security cameras and better outside lighting were in place this time. Officers took turns standing at the door to the event. The orchestra played, a new fundraising record was set again, and there were no eventful happenings all evening, except for a young couple's engagement.

Jodie's parents were at their house to babysit Jake so Joe and Jodie could have a fun evening out. They were enjoying the break, as were Simon and Sally, who also had secured childcare.

Joe smiled as he watched Sissy dancing with her husband, Jon, with a huge smile on her face. She had informed Joe earlier in the day when he had come in for his "little cleanup" at the salon before the dance that their finances—and their marriage—had vastly improved since last Valentine's Day.

Farmerton felt like its old self again—or perhaps an even better version. Maybe even its best version. As Joe twirled one of the two loves of his life around the crowded dance floor, he thought to himself, *Only time will tell.*

The End

Questions for Discussion or Reflection

1. Farmerton has a special tradition on Valentine's Day. Does your community have a holiday for which it goes "all out"? What is it? What if an event like the one Farmerton experienced happened during your community's celebration?

2. Have you ever been surprised to learn about the past of someone you looked up to or admired, like Joe was about Pastor Kate? How did you respond to the revelation?

3. Conrad Kramer seemed to leave a trail of heartbreak and destruction behind him over many years. Do you believe he could really change for good? Do you know someone who has made a significant positive change in their life? How did they achieve it?

4. Conrad had some major issues with his parents, particularly his mother. Do you, or someone you know, have similar struggles?

5. Do you think Billy and Becky were taken advantage of by Genevieve? Who do you think was most responsible for the attempt on the pastor's life, and why?

6. Do you think Pastor Kate is wise to revisit any type of relationship with Conrad, considering its abusive history? Why or why not?

7. This book mentions many types of abusive behaviors. What are some of them? If you, or someone you know, have experienced any of these, what type of help was available, and were you/they able to take advantage of it?

8. What was your biggest "takeaway" from this story?

Author's Note

Matters of the Heart is a work of fiction. All the events, characters, and places in this book are either used fictitiously or are products of my imagination.

Even so, I believe fictional works can examine important truths about real-life situations. They can reveal human emotions and behaviors, both the good and the bad. Stories can also give us hope that things that need changing can indeed successfully change for the better—or, if not, can at least encourage us to remove ourselves from unhealthy situations.

I hope this book might help anyone facing difficult situations or decisions at this time. How will it all work out in the end? Only time will tell.

About Atmosphere Press

Founded in 2015, Atmosphere Press was built on the principles of Honesty, Transparency, Professionalism, Kindness, and Making Your Book Awesome. As an ethical and author-friendly hybrid press, we stay true to that founding mission today.

If you're a reader, enter our giveaway for a free book here:

SCAN TO ENTER
BOOK GIVEAWAY

If you're a writer, submit your manuscript for consideration here:

SCAN TO SUBMIT
MANUSCRIPT

And always feel free to visit Atmosphere Press and our authors online at atmospherepress.com. See you there soon!

About the Author

Matters of the Heart is Kathy J. Jacobson's eighth novel. Her previous publications include the five-book *Noted!* series, as well as the mysteries *In the Secret Heart* and *A Change of Heart*, predecessors to this book.

Kathy lives in Monona, Wisconsin, with her husband. In addition to writing, she enjoys travel, music, theater, sports, and being Grandma Kat.

www.ingramcontent.com/pod-product-compliance
Lightning Source LLC
LaVergne TN
LVHW041927070526
838199LV00051BA/2734